OUT OF THIS WORLD

FICTION

AND

FANTASY

Edited by Deborah H. Sussman

Designed by Marijka Kostiw

COVER ART: Painting by Ron Miller, courtesy of NASA. Artist's conception of what Saturn might look like from Titan, one of Saturn's moons.

ISBN 0-590-35576-7

ACKNOWLEDGMENTS

Grateful acknowledgment is made to the following authors and publishers for the use of copyrighted materials. Every effort has been made to obtain permission to use previously published material. Any errors or omissions are unintentional.

Isaac Asimov for "The Fun They Had" by Isaac Asimov. Copyright © 1951 by NEA Service, Inc. Reprinted by permission of the author.

Arthur C. Clarke for "Trouble with Time" by Arthur C. Clarke. Copyright © 1960 by Davis Publications, Inc. (as "Crime on Mars").

Dell Publishing for "Unready to Wear" by Kurt Vonnegut, Jr. From WELCOME TO THE MONKEY HOUSE by Kurt Vonnegut, Jr. Copyright © 1953 by Kurt Vonnegut, Jr. Reprinted by permission of Delacorte Press / Seymour Lawrence, a division of BANTAM, DOUBLEDAY, DELL PUBLISHING GROUP, INC.

Don Congdon Associates for "Hail and Farewell" by Ray Bradbury, published in TODAY. Reprinted by permission of Don Congdon Associates, Inc. Copyright © 1953 by Ray Bradbury; renewed 1981 by Ray Bradbury. "The Third Level" by Jack Finney, published in COLLIERS. Reprinted by permission of Don Congdon Associates, Inc. Copyright © 1950 by Crowell Collier; renewed 1977 by Jack Finney.

Raymond F. Jones for "A Bowl of Biskies Makes a Growing Boy" by Raymond F. Jones. From THE OTHER SIDE OF TOMORROW, edited by Roger Elwood. Copyright © 1973 by Random House, Inc.

Damon Knight for "To Serve Man" by Damon Knight. Copyright 1950 by GALAXY PUBLISHING CORPORATION.

Ursula K. Le Guin for "The Rule of Names" from THE WIND'S TWELVE QUARTERS by Ursula K. Le Guin. Copyright © 1975 by Ursula K. Le Guin. Originally appeared in FANTASTIC, 1964.

Fritz Leiber for "A Bad Day for Sales" by Fritz Leiber. Copyright © 1953 by GALAXY PUBLISHING CORPORATION.

Scholastic Inc. for "Starlight, Starbright" by Al Nussbaum. Copyright © 1979 by Scholastic Inc.

Scott Meredith Literary Agency, Inc. for "Prone" by Mack Reynolds. Copyright © 1954 by Mercury Press, Inc. From *The Magazine of Fantasy and Science Fiction*. Reprinted by permission of the author and the author's agents, Scott Meredith Literary Agency, Inc., 845 Third Avenue, New York, NY 10022.

Acknowledgments continued on page 160.

CONTENTS

INTRODUCTION

Have you ever wondered if there's life on other planets? Have you ever thought about where you would go if you could travel in time? Or have you ever let your imagination take you to a magical world where anything is possible? If you answered yes to any of these questions, then you have already entered the realm of science fiction and fantasy.

People have been writing science fiction and fantasy for centuries. As far back as 100 A.D., the Greeks were writing stories about going to the moon. And that was almost two thousand years before astronauts landed there!

In this book, we've included some of the best known science fiction and fantasy writers in the world. Isaac Asimov imagines a future without books. Arthur C. Clarke, the man who wrote 2001: A Space Odyssey, *takes a mystery and sets it on another planet. And Ursula K. Le Guin takes us to a land where dragons roam and lizards rule.*

Most of the stories in this book are science fiction; a few of them are fantasy. What's the difference between the two categories? That's a hard question to answer, because the line between them is blurry. But each category does have certain characteristics.

Science fiction describes things that might happen someday in the future. Travel in space is one example, or travel in time. Obviously, nobody has traveled in time yet—at least as far as we know. But there are scientific theories about the possibility.

Fantasy, on the other hand, is less rooted in reality. In Ray Bradbury's "Hail and Farewell," for example, we meet a character who never seems to age. There's no scientific theory to explain his agelessness. It's just a fantastic situation that invites the reader to take a giant leap of imagination.

We hope that all the stories in this book will spark your imagination. We hope they make you think about the world in a new and different way. And most of all, we hope you enjoy reading them.

You've probably heard the expression "The grass is always greener on the other side of the fence." In this story, Isaac Asimov shows us the grass on our side of the fence from a new and different point of view.

THE FUN THEY HAD

ISAAC ASIMOV

Margie even wrote about it that night in her diary. On the page headed May 17, 2155, she wrote, "Today Tommy found a real book."

It was a very old book. Margie's grandfather had heard about books like it when he was a little boy. He once said *his* grandfather had told them that there was a time when all stories were printed on paper.

They turned the pages, which were yellow and crinkly. It was awfully funny to read the words. They stood still, instead of moving the way they were supposed to — on a screen, you know. And then, when they turned back to the page before, it had the same words on it. It was just the same as it had been when they read it the first time.

"Gee," said Tommy. "What a waste. When you're through with the book, you just throw it away, I guess. Our television screen must have had a million books on it, and it's good for plenty more. I wouldn't throw it away."

"Same with mine," said Margie. She was 11 and hadn't seen as many telebooks as Tommy had. He was 13.

She said, "Where did you find it?"

"In my house." He pointed without looking, because he was busy reading. "In the attic."

"What's it about?"

"School."

Margie made a face. "School? What's there to write about

school? I hate school." Margie always hated school, but now she hated it more than ever. The mechanical teacher had been giving her test after test in geography. She had been doing worse and worse. Finally, her mother had shaken her head sadly and sent for the County Inspector.

He was a round little man with a red face. He had a whole box of tools with dials and wires. He smiled at her and gave her an apple. Then he took the teacher apart. Margie had hoped he wouldn't know how to put it together again. But he knew how, all right.

After an hour or so, there it was again — large and black and ugly. It had a big screen, on which all the lessons were shown and the questions were asked. That wasn't so bad. The part she hated most was the slot where she had to put the homework and test papers. She always had to write them out in a punch code they made her learn when she was six years old. The mechanical teacher calculated the mark in no time.

The inspector had smiled after he was finished, and patted her head. He said to her mother, "It's not the little girl's fault, Mrs. Jones. I think the geography sector was geared a little too quick. I've slowed it up to an average 10-year level. Actually, the overall pattern of her progress is quite satisfactory." Again he patted Margie's head.

Margie was disappointed. She had been hoping they would take the teacher away. They had once taken Tommy's teacher away for nearly a month, because the history sector had blanked out.

So she said to Tommy, "Why would anyone write about school?"

Tommy looked at her with superior eyes.

"Because it's not our kind of school, stupid. This is the old kind of school that they had hundreds of years ago." He added, saying the word carefully, "*Centuries* ago."

Margie was hurt. "Well, I don't know what kind of school

they had all that time ago." She read the book over his shoulder for a while. Then she said, "Anyway, they had a teacher."

"Sure they had a teacher, but it wasn't a regular teacher. It was a man."

"A man? How could a man be a teacher?"

"Well, he just told the boys and girls things. He gave them homework and asked them questions."

"A man isn't smart enough."

"Sure he is. My father knows as much as my teacher."

"He can't. A man can't know as much as a teacher."

"He knows almost as much, I betcha."

Margie wasn't prepared to argue. She said, "I wouldn't want a strange man in my house to teach me."

Tommy screamed with laughter. "You don't know much, Margie. The teachers didn't live in the house. They had a special building, and all the kids went there."

"And all the kids learned the same thing?"

"Sure, if they were the same age."

"But my mother says a teacher has to be adjusted to fit the mind of each boy and girl it teaches. Each kid has to be taught differently."

"Just the same, they didn't do it that way then. If you don't like it, you don't have to read the book."

"I didn't say I didn't like it," Margie said quickly. She wanted to read about those funny schools.

They weren't even half finished when Margie's mother called, "Margie! School!"

Margie looked up. "Not yet, Mama."

"Now," said Mrs. Jones. "And it's probably time for Tommy, too."

Margie said to Tommy, "Can I read the book some more with you after school?"

"Maybe," he said. He walked away whistling, the book under his arm.

Margie went into the schoolroom. It was right next to her bedroom. The mechanical teacher was on and waiting for her. It was always on at the same time every day except Saturday and Sunday. Her mother said that little girls learned better if they learned at regular hours.

The screen was lit up. It said, "Today's arithmetic lesson is on the addition of proper fractions. Please insert yesterday's homework in the proper slot."

Margie did so with a sigh. She was thinking about the old schools they had when her grandfather's grandfather was a boy. All the kids from the whole neighborhood came. They laughed and shouted in the schoolroom, and went home together at the end of the day. They learned the same things, so they could help one another with the homework. And they could talk about it.

And the teachers were people. . . .

The mechanical teacher was flashing on the screen: "When we add the fractions 1/2 and 3/4 . . . "

Margie was thinking about how the kids must have loved it in the old days. She was thinking about the fun they had.

The strange visitors from another planet say that they want to help the people of Earth. But no one knows why. Can the visitors be trusted?

TO SERVE MAN

DAMON KNIGHT

The Kanamit were not very pretty, it's true. They looked something like pigs and something like people, and that is not an attractive combination. Seeing them for the first time shocked you.

I don't know what we expected visitors from other planets to look like. Angels, perhaps, or something too strange to be really awful. Maybe that's why we were all so horrified when they landed in their great ships and we saw what they were really like.

The Kanamit were short and very hairy. They had thick, coarse, brown-gray hair all over their plump bodies. Their noses were like pigs' snouts, their eyes were small, and they had thick hands of three fingers each. They wore green leather shorts.

There were three of them at this session of the U.N. I can't tell you how strange it looked to see them there in the middle of a formal session — three fat, piglike creatures in green shorts, surrounded by the delegates from every nation. They politely watched each speaker. Their flat ears hung over the earphones. Later on, I believe, they learned every human language, but at this time they knew only French and English.

They seemed perfectly at ease. That, along with their humor, made me like them. They said quite simply that they wanted to help us. I believed it. As a U.N. translator, of course, my opinion didn't matter. But I thought they were the best thing that ever happened to Earth.

The delegate from Argentina got up and talked about the new cheap power source which the Kanamit had shown us at an earlier session. He said that his government was interested, but could not commit itself without knowing a great deal more.

It was what all the delegates were saying. Janciewicz, the Polish delegate, said almost the same thing. Then the delegate from France introduced Dr. Denis Lévêque, an expert on crime. A lot of equipment was wheeled in.

Dr. Lévêque recalled the question of the delegate from the U.S.S.R. at the earlier session. The delegate had asked, "What is the purpose of the Kanamit? Why are they offering us these gifts, while asking nothing in return?"

The doctor then said, "At the request of several members, we have made a series of tests upon the Kanamit. These tests will now be repeated."

There was a blaze of flashbulbs. One of the TV cameras moved up to focus on the equipment. At the same time, a huge TV screen lighted up. We saw the blank faces of two dials. The pointer of each rested at zero. We saw a strip of paper tape with the point of a marker resting against it.

The doctor's assistants were fastening wires to the head of one of the Kanamit. They wrapped a rubber tube around his forearm, then taped something to the palm of his right hand.

On the screen, we saw the paper tape begin to move. The marker traced a slow zigzag pattern along it. One of the needles began to jump.

"These are the standard instruments for testing the truth of a statement," said Dr. Lévêque. "The bodies and brains of the Kanamit are unknown to us. So our first step was to find out if they react to these tests as human beings do."

He pointed to the first dial. "This instrument measures his brain waves. It has been shown, with humans, that changes in these readings take place when the subject is not speaking the truth."

He picked up two pieces of cardboard. One was red, one was black. The black piece was longer than the red.

"Which of these is longer than the other?" he asked the Kanama.

"The red," said the Kanama.

Both needles leaped wildly. So did the line on the unrolling tape.

"I shall repeat the question," said the doctor. "Which of these is longer?"

"The black," said the creature.

The needles did not jump.

"How did you come to this planet?" asked the doctor.

"Walked," said the Kanama.

Again, the instruments leaped. There was laughter among the delegates.

"Once more," said the doctor. "How did you come to this planet?"

"In a spaceship," said the Kanama. The instruments did not jump.

The doctor faced the delegates.

"Many such experiments were made," he said. "They proved that our equipment works. Now I shall ask our guest to reply to the question from the Soviet delegate. Why are the Kanamit people offering these great gifts to the people of Earth?"

The Kanama rose. In English, he said, "I hope that the people of Earth will understand and believe that our mission is simple. It is to bring to you the peace and plenty that *we* enjoy. We have, in the past, brought it to other races throughout the galaxy. When your world has no more hunger, no more war, no more suffering — that will be our reward."

And the needles had not jumped once.

The delegate from the Ukraine jumped to his feet. He asked to be allowed to speak. But the time was up, and the

Secretary-General closed the session.

I met my fellow translator Grigori as we were leaving the U.N. chamber. His face was red with excitement. "Who dreamed up that circus?" he asked.

"The tests looked real to me," I said.

"A circus!" he said. "A joke! If they were real, Peter, why was there no debate?"

"There will be time for debate tomorrow, surely."

"Tomorrow the doctor and his machine will be back in Paris. Lots can happen before tomorrow. Man, how can anybody trust a thing that looks as if it ate the baby?"

I was a little angry. "Are you sure you're not more worried about their politics than the way they look?" I said.

He said, "Bah," and went away.

The next day, reports came in from laboratories all over the world. The Kanamit's power source had been tested. Those little metal boxes would give more power than atomic energy. They would cost next to nothing and last nearly forever. They were so cheap to make that everybody in the world could have one of his own. By afternoon, 17 countries had begun to set up factories to turn them out.

The next day, the Kanamit turned up with a machine that would increase the amount of food that could grow in any land by 60 to 100 percent. The day after that, they dropped their bombshell.

"You now have a future with unlimited power and food," said one of them. He pointed with his three-fingered hand to a box on the table before him. It had a reflector on the front of it. "We offer you today a third gift."

He waved to the TV men to roll their cameras over. Then he picked up a large sheet of cardboard. It was covered with drawings and English words. We saw it on the large screen.

"This broadcast is going all over your world," said the Kanama. "I hope that everyone who can take pictures from TV screens will use their cameras now. This machine creates a field in which nothing, of any kind, can explode."

There was silence.

The Kanama said, "It cannot be kept from anyone now. If one nation has it, all must have it." When nobody seemed to understand, he said, "There will be no more war."

That was the biggest news in 1,000 years. It turned out that the explosions included the ones in gasoline and diesel engines. They had made it impossible for anybody to equip a modern army.

We could have gone back to bows and arrows, of course, but that wouldn't have satisfied the military. Besides, there wouldn't be any reason to make war. Every nation would soon have everything.

Nobody ever gave another thought to those lie-detector tests. Grigori was annoyed; he had nothing to prove his suspicions were right.

I quit my job with the U.N. a few months later, because I saw there was going to be nothing for the U.N. to do. Every nation on Earth was well on the way to being self-supporting.

I took a job as translator with the Kanamit Embassy, and it was there that I ran into Grigori again. I was glad to see him, but I couldn't imagine what he was doing there.

"I thought you were on the other side," I said. "Don't tell me you think the Kanamit are all right now."

"I still hate the looks of them," he said. "You were right, of course — they mean us nothing but good. But do you know — the question of the Soviet delegate was never answered. They told us what they wanted to do — 'to bring you the peace and plenty that *we* enjoy.' But they didn't say *why*."

"Why do missionaries —"

"Missionaries do it for religious reasons. If these creatures have a religion, they've never said anything about it. Now, what will the Kanamit people gain from helping us?"

I said, "Learning —"

"No, it's not as clear as that. It's something strange. Something to do with their way of thinking, not ours. But trust me, Peter. There is no such thing as doing good just for its own sake. In one way or another, they have something to gain."

"And that's why you're here," I said, "to try to find out what it is?"

"Right. I wanted to get on one of the 10-year exchange groups to their home planet, but I couldn't. They were filled up in a week. Instead, I'm studying their language. Language shows the basic thinking of the people who use it. I've learned a lot of the spoken words already. It's not hard, really, and there are hints in it. Some of the expressions are a lot like English. I'm sure I'll get the answer in the end."

"More power to you," I said, and went back to work.

I saw Grigori often from then on. He was highly excited about a month after that first meeting. He'd got hold of a book of the Kanamit, and was trying to read it. Their word signs were harder than Chinese, but he said he would work it out if it took years. He wanted my help.

I was interested, though I knew it would be a long job. We worked with notes from Kanamit bulletin boards and things like that. We also had the little English-Kanamit dictionary they gave the staff. I worried about the stolen book, but as time went by I got deeper into the problem. Languages are my field, after all. I couldn't help being interested.

We got the title worked out in a few weeks. It was *How to Serve Man*. It seemed to be a handbook they were giving out to new Kanamit staff members. New ones were coming in all the time now. They were opening all kinds of clinics, and so on. If there was anybody on Earth who didn't trust them — besides Grigori — he must have been in a cave somewhere.

It was amazing to see the changes in less than a year. There were no more armies. There was enough of everything. There was no unemployment. When you picked up a newspaper, you didn't see "H-bomb" or "Satellite" leaping out at you. The news was always good. The Kanamit had found ways to make the human race taller, stronger, and healthier. We would be almost a race of supermen. They were finding cures for heart disease and cancer.

I didn't see Grigori for two weeks after we worked out the title of the book. I was on vacation in Canada. When I got back, I was shocked by the change in him.

"What on earth is wrong, Grigori?" I asked. "You look terrible."

"Come down to the bar."

I went with him, and he drank a stiff Scotch as if he needed it.

"Come on, man, what's the matter?" I said.

"The Kanamit have put me on the list for the next exchange ship," he said. "You, too, or I wouldn't be talking to you."

"Well," I said, "but —"

"They're not doing good for its own sake."

I tried to reason with him. I pointed out that they had made Earth a paradise, compared to what it was before. He only shook his head.

Then I said, "Well, what about those lie-detector tests?"

"A joke," he answered calmly. "I said so at the time, you fool. They told the truth, though, as far as it went."

"And the book?" I said. "What about that? *How to Serve Man*? That wasn't put there for you to read. They *mean* it. How do you explain that?"

"I've read the first paragraph of that book," he said. "Why do you suppose I haven't slept for a week?"

I said, "Well?" and he smiled a strange, twisted smile.

"It's a cookbook," he said.

Lacy can't imagine what her father thinks about when he stares at the brightest star in the sky. But then, Lacy and her father are from two very different worlds.

STARLIGHT, STARBRIGHT

AL NUSSBAUM

Lacy left for the fields with her father shortly before dawn. When their huge tractor reached their work spot, a pink sun was peeking over the horizon. Their two fuzzy shadows stretched far over the flat ground. They were able to work without talking. Each knew what had to be done.

In fact, it was the machine the tractor pulled that did most of the work. The father had to drive the tractor at the proper speed and over the right ground. And Lacy had to make sure the machine was supplied with the seed, water, and special fertilizer it needed.

The machine did everything else. It tilled the rust-colored soil. It sowed the seed, and tested the ground so that just the right amount of fertilizer was added. Then it gave the seeds their first sprinkle of water and smoothed everything over.

Later, the machine would also harvest the crop and prepare it for long-term storage by canning or freezing. The machine had cost a fortune, but it was worth it.

Suddenly, the tractor lost power and stopped. Lacy knew her father's wrist alarm must have gone off. It had told him it was time to rest. Lacy climbed down from the machine and walked toward the tractor. Her father joined her on the ground just as her brother came racing up with their lunch. They sat together on the ground beside the tractor to eat.

"Craig," Lacy's father said, "it's a good thing we're not back in Illinois. The way you drive, you'd knock down all the trees in the state."

Craig smiled. "That's what you always say. No matter where we go, you and Mom always say it's a good thing we're not in Illinois. But I don't think you mean it."

"I mean it, all right. This spot isn't perfect. The soil is too dry and the air is too thin, but it's ours. All ours. We have ten thousand acres of the best. By the time we die, we'll have built up a fine farm for Lacy and you. That's what my parents did for me and their parents did for them."

The father paused a moment, then continued. "If the cities hadn't kept getting bigger, using more and more farmland as they grew, we'd still be in Illinois. But we had to sell our land to make room for a city, and now this is the best place for us. We're right where we should be."

"You could have switched to hydroponics," Craig suggested. "That's what I would have done."

"That's not farming!" his father exploded. "Growing a crop in a tank of water and chemicals isn't natural."

"But," Craig insisted, "the people who do it are producing a lot with very little space."

"I would sooner have gone to New Detroit and slaved away my twenty-two hour work week for someone else — making monorails, or something."

"Do you mean that?"

"All you have to do is look around you. We're here. If I were not the kind of man who means what he says, we wouldn't be here."

Craig drove back to the house, leaving Lacy and their father in the field. There was still some work to do before they stopped for the day. But Lacy's father did not get up to begin again. Instead, he stayed where he was, sitting on the ground with his back against the side of the tractor.

All at once, Lacy saw what the trouble was. Her father was staring at the star again. It was always the brightest spot in the sky except for the sun. It could be seen even when it appeared in the daylight.

"What do you think about when you look at that star?" Lacy asked.

"It's not a star. It's a planet," Lacy's father replied. "I taught you that much."

"Well, you know what I mean. What do you think about?"

"I think about Illinois," her father said in a faraway voice. "I think about home and what it would be like to feel wind and rain on my face. It would be hard not to think about Earth when I'm watching it move across the sky."

"Why don't I feel that way?" Lacy asked.

"Maybe it's because you weren't born on Earth like Craig, your mom, and I. You were born here." Lacy's father smiled as though he had thought of something pleasant. "You're a Martian," he said.

Have you ever wondered what it would be like if you could stay young forever? In this story, Ray Bradbury takes a bittersweet look at what might happen if you could.

HAIL AND FAREWELL

RAY BRADBURY

But of course he was going away; there was nothing else to do; the time was up; the clock had run out, and he was going very far away indeed. His suitcase was packed; his shoes were shined; his hair was brushed; he had expressly washed behind his ears; and it remained only for him to go down the stairs, out the front door, and up the street to the small-town station where the train would make a stop for him alone. Then Fox Hill, Illinois, would be left far off in his past. And he would go on, perhaps to Iowa, perhaps to Kansas, perhaps even to California; a small boy, twelve years old, with a birth certificate in his valise to show he had been born forty-three years ago.

"Willie!" called a voice downstairs.

"Yes!" He hoisted his suitcase. In his bureau mirror he saw a face made of June dandelions and July apples and warm summer-morning milk. There, as always, was his look of the angel and the innocent, which might never, in the years of his life, change.

"Almost time," called the woman's voice.

"All right!" And he went down the stairs, grunting and smiling. In the living room sat Anna and Steve, their clothes painfully neat.

"Here I am!" cried Willie in the parlor door.

Anna looked like she was going to cry. "Oh, good Lord, you can't really be leaving us, can you, Willie?"

"People are beginning to talk," said Willie quietly. "I've

been here three years now. But when people begin to talk, I know it's time to put on my shoes and buy a railway ticket."

"It's all so strange. I don't understand. It's so sudden," Anna said. "Willie, we'll miss you."

"I'll write you every Christmas, so help me. Don't you write me."

"It's been a great pleasure and satisfaction," said Steve, sitting there, his words the wrong size in his mouth. "It's a shame it had to stop. It's a shame you had to tell us about yourself. It's an awful shame you can't stay on."

"You're the nicest folks I ever had," said Willie, four feet high, in no need of a shave, the sunlight on his face.

And then Anna *did* cry. "Willie, Willie." And she sat down and looked as if she wanted to hold him but was afraid to hold him now; she looked at him with shock and amazement and her hands empty, not knowing what to do with him now.

"It's not easy to go," said Willie. "You get used to things. You want to stay. But it doesn't work. I tried to stay on once after people began to suspect. 'How horrible!' people said. 'All these years, playing with our innocent children,' they said, 'and us not guessing! Awful!' they said. And finally I had to just leave town one night. It's not easy. You know darned well how much I love both of you. Thanks for three swell years."

They all went to the front door. "Willie, where're you going?"

"I don't know. I just start traveling. When I see a town that looks green and nice, I settle in."

"Will you ever come back?"

"Yes," he said earnestly with his high voice. "In about twenty years it should begin to show in my face. When it does, I'm going to make a grand tour of all the mothers and fathers I've ever had."

They stood on the cool summer porch, reluctant to say the last words. Steve was looking steadily at an elm tree. "How many other folks've you stayed with, Willie? How many adoptions?"

Willie figured it, pleasantly enough. "I guess it's about five towns and five couples and over twenty years gone by since I started my tour."

"Well, we can't holler," said Steve. "Better to've had a son thirty-six months than none whatever."

"Well," said Willie, and kissed Anna quickly, seized at his luggage, and was gone up the street in the green noon light, under the trees, a very young boy indeed, not looking back, running steadily.

The boys were playing on the green park diamond when he came by. He stood a little while among the oak-tree shadows, watching them hurl the white, snowy baseball into the warm summer air, saw the baseball shadow fly like a dark bird over the grass, saw their hands open in mouths to catch this swift piece of summer that now seemed most especially important to hold on to. The boys' voices yelled. The ball lit on the grass near Willie.

Carrying the ball forward from under the shade trees, he thought of the last three years now spent to the penny, and the five years before that, and so on down the line to the year when he was really eleven and twelve and fourteen and the voices saying: "What's wrong with Willie, missus?" "Mrs. B., is Willie late a-growin'?" "Willie, you smokin' cigars lately?" The echoes died in summer light and color. His mother's voice: "Willie's twenty-one today!" And a thousand voices saying: "Come back, son, when you're fifteen; *then* maybe we'll give you a job."

He stared at the baseball in his trembling hand, as if it were his life, an interminable ball of years strung around and around and around, but always leading back to his twelfth birthday. He heard the kids walking toward him; he felt them blot out the sun, and they were older, standing around him.

"Willie! Where you goin'?" They kicked his suitcase.

How tall they stood in the sun. In the last few months it seemed the sun had passed a hand above their heads, beckoned, and they were warm metal drawn melting upward; they were golden taffy pulled by an immense gravity to the sky, thirteen, fourteen years old, looking down upon Willie, smiling, but already beginning to neglect him. It had started four months ago:

"Choose up sides! Who wants Willie?"

"Aw, Willie's too little; we don't play with 'kids.'"

And they raced ahead of him, drawn by the moon and the sun and the turning seasons of leaf and wind, and he was twelve years old and not of them anymore. And the other voices beginning again on the old, the dreadfully familiar, the cool refrain: "Better feed that boy vitamins, Steve." "Anna, does shortness *run* in your family?" And the cold fist knocking at your heart again and knowing that the roots would have to be pulled up again after so many good years with the "folks."

"Willie, where you goin'?"

He jerked his head. He was back among the towering, shadowing boys who milled around him like giants at a drinking fountain bending down.

"Goin' a few days visitin' a cousin of mine."

"Oh." There was a day, a year ago, when they would have cared very much indeed. But now there was only curiosity for his luggage, their enchantment with trains and trips and far places.

"How about a coupla fast ones?" said Willie.

They looked doubtful, but, considering the circumstances, nodded. He dropped his bag and ran out; the white baseball was up in the sun, away to their burning white figures in the far meadow, up in the sun again, rushing, life coming and going in a pattern. Here, *there*! Mr. and Mrs. Robert Hanlon, Creek Bend, Wisconsin, 1932, the first couple, the first year!

Here, *there*! Henry and Alice Boltz, Limeville, Iowa, 1935! The baseball flying. The Smiths, the Eatons, the Robinsons! 1939! 1945! Husband and wife, husband and wife, husband and wife, no children, no children! A knock on this door, a knock on that.

"Pardon me. My name is William. I wonder if —"

"A sandwich? Come in, sit down. Where you *from*, son?"

The sandwich, a tall glass of cold milk, the smiling, the nodding, the comfortable, leisurely talking.

"Son, you look like you been traveling. You run *off* from somewhere?"

"No."

"Boy, are you an orphan?"

Another glass of milk.

"We always wanted kids. It never worked out. Never knew why. One of those things. Well, well. It's getting late, son. Don't you think you better hit for home?"

"Got no home."

"A boy like you? Not dry behind the ears? Your mother'll be worried."

"Got no home and no folks anywhere in the world. I wonder if — I wonder — could I sleep here tonight?"

"Well, now, son, I don't just know. We never considered taking in —" said the husband.

"We got chicken for supper tonight," said the wife, "enough for extras, enough for company. . . ."

And the years turning and flying away, the voices, and the faces, and the people, and always the same first conversations. The voice of Emily Robinson, in her rocking chair, in summer-night darkness, the last night he stayed with her, the night she discovered his secret, her voice saying:

"I look at all the little children's faces going by. And I sometimes think, What a shame, what a shame, that all these flowers have to be cut, all these bright fires have to be put out. What a shame these, all of these you see in schools or running by, have to get tall and unsightly and wrinkle and turn gray or get bald, and finally, all bone and wheeze, be dead and buried off away. When I hear them laugh I can't believe they'll ever go the road I'm going. Yet here they *come*! I still remember Wordsworth's poem: 'When all at once I saw a crowd, A host of golden daffodils; Beside the lake, beneath the trees, Fluttering and dancing in the breeze.' That's how I think of children, cruel as they sometimes are, mean as I know they can be, but not yet showing the meanness around their eyes or *in* their eyes, not yet full of tiredness. They're so eager for everything! I guess that's what I miss most in older folks, the eagerness gone nine times out of ten, the freshness gone, so much of the drive and life down the drain. I like to watch school let out each day. It's like someone threw a bunch of flowers out the school front doors. How does it feel, Willie? How does it feel to be young forever? To look like a silver dime new from the mint? Are you happy? Are you as fine as you *seem*?"

The baseball whizzed from the blue sky, stung his hand like a great pale insect. Nursing it, he hears his memory say:

"I worked with what I had. After my folks died, after I found I couldn't get man's work anywhere, I tried carnivals, but they only laughed. 'Son,' they said, 'you're not a midget, and even if you are, you look like a *boy*! We want midgets with midgets' *faces*! Sorry, son, sorry.' So I left home, started out, thinking: What *was* I? A boy. I looked like a boy, sounded like a boy, so I might as well go on being a boy. No use fighting it. No use screaming. So what could I do? What job was handy? And then one day I saw this man in a restaurant looking at another man's pictures of his children. 'Sure wish I had kids,' he said. 'Sure wish I had kids.' He kept shaking his head. And me sitting a few seats away from him, a hamburger in my hands. I sat there, *frozen*! At that very instant I knew what my job would be for all the rest of my life. There *was* work for me, after all. Making lonely people happy. Keeping myself busy. Playing forever. I knew I had to play forever. Deliver a few papers, run a few errands, mow a few lawns, maybe. But hard work? No. All I had to do was be a mother's son and a father's pride. I turned to the man down the counter from me. 'I beg your pardon,' I said. I *smiled* at him. . . ."

"But, Willie," said Mrs. Emily long ago, "didn't you ever get lonely? Didn't you ever want — *things* — that grown-ups wanted?"

"I fought that out alone," said Willie. "I'm a boy, I told myself, I'll have to live in a boy's world, read boys' books, play boys' games, cut myself off from everything else. I can't be both. I got to be only one thing — young. And so I played that way. Oh, it wasn't easy. There were times —" He lapsed into silence.

"And the family you lived with, they never knew?"

"No. Telling them would have spoiled everything. I told them I was a runaway; I let them check through official channels, police. Then, when there was no record, let them put in to adopt me. That was best of all; as long as they never guessed. But then, after three years, or five years, they guessed, or a traveling man came through, or a carnival man saw me, and it was over. It always had to end."

"And you're very happy and it's nice being a child for over forty years?"

"It's a living, as they say. And when you make other people happy, then you're almost happy, too. I got my job to do and I do it. And anyway, in a few years now I'll be in my second childhood. All the fevers will be out of me and all the unfulfilled things and most of the dreams. Then I can relax, maybe, and play the role all the way."

He threw the baseball one last time and broke the reverie. Then he was running to seize his luggage. Tom, Bill, Jamie,

Bob, Sam — their names moved on his lips. They were embarrassed at his shaking hands.

"After all, Willie, it ain't as if you're going to China or Timbuktu."

"That's right, isn't it?" Willie did not move.

"So long, Willie. See you next week!"

"So long, so long!"

And he was walking off with his suitcase again, looking at the trees, going away from the boys and the street where he had lived, and as he turned the corner a train whistle screamed, and he began to run.

The last thing he saw and heard was a white ball tossed at a high roof, back and forth, back and forth, and two voices crying out as the ball pitched now up, down, and back through the sky. "Annie, Annie, over! Annie, Annie, over!" like the crying of birds flying off to the far south.

In the early morning, with the smell of the mist and the cold metal, with the iron smell of the train around him and a full night of traveling shaking his bones and his body, and a smell of the sun beyond the horizon, he awoke and looked out upon a small town just arising from sleep. Lights were coming on, soft voices muttered, a red signal bobbed back and forth, back and forth in the cold air. There was that sleeping hush in which echoes are dignified by clarity, in which echoes stand nakedly alone and sharp. A porter moved by, a shadow in shadows.

"Sir," said Willie.

The porter stopped.

"What town's this?" whispered the boy in the dark.

"Valleyville."

"How many people?"

"Ten thousand. Why? This your stop?"

"It looks green." Willie gazed out at the cold morning town for a long time. "It looks nice and quiet," said Willie.

"Son," said the porter, "you know where you *going*?"

"Here," said Willie, and got up quietly in the still, cool, iron-smelling morning, in the train dark, with a rustling and stir.

"I hope you know what you're doing, boy," said the porter.

"Yes, sir," said Willie. "I know what I'm doing." And he was down the dark aisle, luggage lifted after him by the porter, and out in the smoking, steaming-cold, beginning-to-lighten morning. He stood looking up at the porter and the black metal train against the few remaining stars. The train gave a great wailing blast of whistle, the porters cried out all along the line, the cars jolted, and his special porter waved and smiled down at the boy there, the small boy there with the big luggage who shouted up to him, even as the whistle screamed again.

"What?" shouted the porter, hand cupped to ear.

"Wish me luck!" cried Willie.

"Best of luck, son," called the porter, waving, smiling. "Best of luck, boy!"

"Thanks," said Willie, in the great sound of the train, in the steam and roar.

He watched the black train until it was completely gone away and out of sight. He did not move all the time it was going. He stood quietly, a small boy twelve years old, on the worn wooden platform, and only after three entire minutes did he turn at last to face the empty streets below.

Then, as the sun was rising, he began to walk very fast, so as to keep warm, down into the new town.

George Williams stumbles upon a chilling discovery —
one so dangerous that he may not live to tell the tale.

A BOWL OF BISKIES
MAKES A GROWING BOY

RAYMOND F. JONES

George Williams supposed he had read the free offers, the
list of ingredients, and the recipe for Biskie cookies printed
on the sides of the Biskie boxes at least nine thousand times.
He had been eating Biskies for breakfast as long as he could
remember. He must have liked them at one time, but he
didn't know how that was possible. They tasted like sawdust
with blackstrap molasses.

He remembered when he used to save the box tops and
send in for a toy computer that always gave wrong answers,
a water pistol that leaked all over his drawer, and even once
a real live turtle that arrived dead.

That had been a long time ago. He had quit sending in box
tops when he was twelve. But he still read the Biskie box over
and over. There wasn't anything else to stare at each morning
as he munched the woody-tasting stuff. He wished his mother
would cook breakfast sometime, but he was sure she didn't
know how. When he said he was tired of Biskies she came
up with something even worse — sawdust with white crystals
that looked like the mold you found when you turned over
a rotten log in the woods. It was called Sweet Sparkles or
some idiotic name like that.

This morning was no different. His father had the morning
paper in the living room. His mother was in the bathroom
doing something to her face before she went to her job. His
two sisters were knocking down the walls with their stereo
blasts.

George read the stuff on the sides of the Biskie box.

They must have gone to a new ad agency, he thought. The artist who drew the Biskie Boy was making him look more like an undernourished orphan with every new batch of boxes. But the caption over him still read, "Hey, fellows! A bowl of Biskies makes a growing boy!"

George read the list of vitamins and noted that the minimum daily requirements of B-12 had not been established. He wondered why somebody didn't get busy and establish it. That might make a good project for a master's degree when he got to college.

But that was a long way off. The immediate problem was to get through his senior year of high school without climbing the walls with boredom. His only relief was his own biochemistry lab, which his folks had let him set up in the basement levels of the city-building. It cost them extra rent, but they didn't object. He was grateful to them.

He read on down through the fine print at the bottom of the Biskie box. It didn't seem possible, but there seemed to be some stuff there he hadn't noticed before in all his years of reading the boxes. It had to do with what Biskies were made of: Oats, corn, wheat germ, soya, seaweed, dried milk, flavoring (where!) — and sodium propionate, bisulphide of lime, and potassium metathorinate as preservatives. The cereal ought to last at least five thousand years with all that crap in it.

It was a wonder the box didn't explode.

In disgust, he noted the clock showed he was nearly late again. He'd lost his appetite already, so it didn't matter. He got up from the table, leaving the bowl half filled with Biskies and their load of sodium propionate, bisulphide of lime, and potassium metathorinate. He grabbed his briefcase of books and papers, waved good-by to his indifferent family, and raced out to catch the escalator to the school halls on the ninety-fifth floor.

Potassium metathorinate.

The name of the chemical spun in his mind. At higher floors, the escalator was jammed with other students, who funneled wildly onto it with 90-decibel yakking and brutal horseplay. Usually he joined in their jostling, in self-defense if nothing else, but he kept thinking this morning of potassium metathorinate. He knew he had read something about the chemical at one time.

Something bad.

He got off the escalator at the library floor and decided to skip math, his first class. After a half-hour of searching in the library he found the article in a chemical journal from a couple of years earlier. The article was as he remembered it. It said that potassium metathorinate had been determined to have a definite long-lasting hallucinogenic threshold.

This was what the Biskie Company used as a preservative.

George sat at the table for a long time, staring through the window at the distant city-buildings. He studied the article closely, reading it over and over. The researchers described how the ingestion of potassium metathorinate could leave a patient wide open to any dramatization going on around him. He would latch on to any forceful personality in the show and drop his own identity, literally becoming another person for a long period. George thought of the effect of watching TV after having loaded up with potassium metathorinate.

The possibilities frightened him. He had eaten tons of Biskies in his time. Fortunately, he almost never watched TV.

He decided to approach Professor Thompson, head of the Chemistry Department, who had helped him so much in his basement lab studies. As the class period ended, he took the escalator to the science floor.

"Come in, George," Professor Thompson said heartily as George approached the open door of the office. "How is that cytoplasm experiment coming along at home?"

"It's working out fine," said George. "I know you've got another class, but I wanted to ask you about something I found. I don't understand it."

"Sure. Come in and show me what you have."

Professor Thompson was a ruddy, cheerful man who seemed positive that all of life's problems were little ones. He took the journal and glanced at the article George pointed out.

He looked up after reading it. "It's an interesting item. What puzzles you about it?"

"Did you know that the breakfast food called Biskies uses potassium metathorinate as a preservative?"

Professor Thompson's face sobered. "No, 1 can't say that I did."

"That's the truth. It's listed on the box. How could this company be using a dangerous chemical like that as a preservative? I don't see how it could happen in this modern age."

Professor Thompson closed the journal and handed it back to George. He beamed again, recovering from his momentary seriousness. "We've studied these things extensively in class. You know how the components of manufactured products are controlled by the Government today. You can answer your own question, can't you, George?"

"The answer should be that the article is wrong. These researchers reached some wrong conclusions. The Government wouldn't allow use of the chemical if it were dangerous."

"You've answered your own question."

George hesitated. "But what if — what if somehow these researchers are right? What if somebody in the Government has made a mistake or become careless? This could be a terribly serious thing."

Professor Thompson's face sobered again. He placed his hands on George's shoulders and looked him in the eyes. "It could indeed be serious — if you persist in that kind of thinking, George. You answered the question correctly when you said you didn't see how such a thing could happen in this modern age. It couldn't. The Government doesn't make mistakes of that magnitude. I could tell you of the hundreds of interlocking controls they have to prevent such things from happening, but I don't have the time.

"The most serious part of the matter arises only if you allow yourself to ask such questions. Carelessness of this nature has not happened in your lifetime, or mine, or your parents'. If you allow yourself to be caught up in such doubts, you'll find yourself capable of disloyalty, lack of diligence. You could even be accused of Naderism."

George knew the term. It referred to the man who had become the classic enemy of economic progress in his own time. His wild persecutions of economic producers almost destroyed the economy of a generation. Naderism was equivalent to economic — if not political — treason.

"It's dangerous," Professor Thompson continued. "This chemical, potassium metathorinate, is in authorized use in a product distributed under Government license. It can't be questioned without harm to yourself. That's a major lesson you must learn in the field of scientific inquiry.

"Obviously, the researchers who wrote this report are wrong. I suspect they have long ago disappeared from the scientific scene. Remember this lesson, and remember it well, George. And get that misleading journal out of your hands and back to the library files."

"I will. Thanks a lot, Professor, for your time and help."

George returned the journal to the library and went to his classes for the rest of the day. He was still troubled, however. Somebody had made a mistake. Was there complete certainty that it was the researchers?

He recognized the treacherous ground on which he

walked. Even an accusation of Naderism could destroy a person's career. He slept little that night. At breakfast he avoided Biskies and ate some bread and jam. Then he noticed the label on the jam bottle. Potassium metathorinate was a preservative in the jam.

A tightness clutched his stomach. Careful not to disturb his family, he searched the kitchen shelves and read the fine print on all the labels. The chemical was in pickles, butter, precooked foods — in everything he found except canned spinach.

When he reached school he went immediately to the library to get the chemical journal again. He wanted to find out who the researchers were and their credentials. He had forgotten the call number and had to check the card index again. He let the tape roll rapidly, flashing the entries on the viewing screen. Irritated, he realized he had gone past his point, and pushed the re-roll control. Once again he searched, this time more slowly. He blinked in disbelief. He knew he was looking at the same tape he'd had the previous day, but the entry was no longer there.

He loosened the neck of his shirt, which had become suddenly too warm.

If only he hadn't been careless with the number he had written the day before. He searched his case and his books again. It had to be there somewhere —

It was. He breathed in relief and went to the chute where periodicals were obtained. He punched the call number on the keyboard and waited.

In a moment a small red-lettered notice appeared on the information screen: *The number you have requested is not assigned to any document in the library. Please recheck the card catalog and enter the correct number.*

He glanced at the slip in his hand. Yesterday that number had gotten him the journal with the potassium metathorinate article.

He approached the girl at the information desk. She smiled pleasantly at him. "May I help you?"

He held out the slip. "I checked out a magazine, a chemical journal, on this number yesterday. Today the machine says there's nothing in the library on that number."

Still smiling, the girl took the slip and punched the buttons on her own keyboard. She glanced at the response and gave a little frown. "It's not a valid number. You'll have to check the card index again."

"It's not in the card index today, either."

"Well, then —" She smiled as if he were a little child. "You couldn't possibly have gotten that journal here yesterday or at any other time, could you?"

"I did," he said. "Somebody's taken it out of the library and erased it from the index since yesterday because they didn't want that material read anymore."

Her smile vanished. "That's ridiculous. You know that, don't you? Things like that just don't happen. You can only get yourself in trouble by saying things like that."

"I'm sorry." George clutched the slip and moved away to one of the work tables between shelves. He sat down, feeling a little sick to his stomach. Professor Thompson was the only one he had spoken to about the metathorinate article. So the Professor must have reported him — to somebody who had authority to remove a document from the library files.

Now his persistent inquiry today would be entered in his files. The librarian would not fail to note his assumption that the document had been removed to keep him from reading it.

George borrowed Biskies from the boys on all of the twenty floors of the city-building assigned to his school. He brought home a few boxes each day, saying that his mother had run out of the cereal and that he'd replace theirs in a few days. None of the boys really expected him to return the loan. After all, a box or two of Biskies was nothing.

He accumulated about three hundred boxes in the basement lab. He'd read that potassium metathorinate was water soluble, so it was a simple matter to leach it out of the Biskies with distilled water. He got a lot of other stuff, too, but at least he was rid of the compost the Biskie Company sold as breakfast food with Government sanction. He flushed that down the toilet, a few gobs at a time.

He set up a low-temperature distillation rig that he ran continually to reduce the liquid volume. Then he set out to figure a way to isolate the potassium metathorinate. It took him four weeks, but at the end of that time he had a tenth of a gram of the pure chemical.

This was the only safe way he knew to obtain a supply of potassium metathorinate. He could, of course, have purchased some at a chemical supply house, but that purchase would have gone immediately into the computer-stored history of his life's activities. Combined with the report which Professor Thompson had undoubtedly entered on his school record, and the accusation he had made to the librarian — this would have produced a red card in somebody's file. A red card with the name of George Williams on it. And he would have been called into somebody's office for questioning, and restrictions would have been made concerning places he could go, classes he could take in school, material he could read in the library. He didn't know what else might result, but he knew the bars would go up.

Based on the amount of metathorinate he had recovered, and allowing for losses in his processing, he estimated that a person eating a box of Biskies a week would ingest about two milligrams of the chemical per month. He decided to test an intake of ten milligrams, although he had no real guidelines as to a maximum permissible dose. He mixed the chemical with powdered sugar in his laboratory mixer so that a level teaspoonful of sugar provided a ten-milligram dose.

He swallowed it as soon as he arrived home from school the following afternoon. He had no idea what to expect — unconsciousness, illness, or visions of fiery demons in the air. He lay down on a sofa in his small library and waited for results. Tired after the boring day at school, he went to sleep for about an hour.

Nothing happened.

Maybe he had been completely wrong, after all. Maybe Professor Thompson had been right. The removal of the journal from the library was justified. What a fool he had made of himself if this were true!

After dinner was over and the disposable tableware had been scooped into the central disposal that serviced the building, the family settled down for its evening of TV. There were three screens. The girls latched on to one for their music and personality shows. Their mother chose one for her evening soap opera. George joined his father for westerns and mystery.

His father was pleased. George usually disappeared into his basement laboratory or went to the baseball floor in the evening. The prospect of his son's company cheered Mr. Williams, who usually spent the evening alone in front of the screen.

"You'll like this one tonight," said Mr. Williams. "In fact, we've got three good ones. First is Rick Davis, Range Marshall. He's working to get Mr. Callum, the big land baron, not to foreclose on the Patrick ranch. We'll have to see whether he makes it or not."

George lounged on the floor, his head against a massive pillow. He wished he could understand why his family shut themselves in the cells of their rooms for hours every night to watch the screen fantasies. He hoped he could bear watching long enough to test the hypotheses presented by the report on potassium metathorinate in the chemical journal.

To his surprise, George found himself becoming absorbed

in the story. Mr. Callum, the land baron, was a vicious character. He had foreclosed the ranch Hap Patrick and his young wife had struggled so hard to settle. Now they were on the verge of making it a success, but a bad winter had left their herds depleted, and they couldn't realize enough from the spring sale to make payment on the mortgage. Mr. Callum was forcing them out.

Somebody ought to kill him, George thought. He felt as if he knew exactly how Hap Patrick felt. You work until your back breaks to get a step up the ladder, and then somebody like Callum comes along and kicks you in the teeth. The Callums of the world didn't deserve to live.

George's father had a cold beer during the commercial. George found the commercial interesting, however. He was almost persuaded to run out and buy the stomach medicine offered by the smooth salesman on the screen.

The second part of the show began to reveal a new aspect of the Callum-Patrick situation. Marshall Davis had just prevented Hap from shooting Callum, which George thought was stupid. But then it developed that Mr. Callum had suffered severe problems, too. The railroad had taken a good portion of his land at prices much lower than he considered fair. And he wanted a ranch on which to settle his old father and mother. His father had been a cattleman all his life and knew nothing else. He needed a good ranch to finish out his life.

George found himself suddenly sympathizing with Mr. Callum. He wasn't a coal-black villain, after all. He was a rather sad victim of circumstance, trying to do the best he could.

Hap Patrick, on the other hand, wasn't really happy with ranch life. He'd done the best he could, but he had made serious mistakes because his heart wasn't in it. As the railroad agents came through, he got a good job as a foreman with the rail crews, and he was much happier.

When the show was over, everybody was happy, and George felt stirred as he had never been stirred before. It was so overwhelming that he felt he couldn't take any more for the night.

"That was a good show," he said to his father. "I thought for a while there that Callum ought to be hung. But he wasn't such a bad guy, after all."

Mr. Williams nodded happily. "I'm glad you enjoyed it. I like Rick Davis myself, but he didn't have too much to do tonight. Don't go away. You'll like the next two. Mason is next. That's a good detective story."

"Thanks, Dad, but I've got some studying, and I want to get to bed early. It's a big day tomorrow."

"Sure. Wish you could stay. I'll tell you about the best one at breakfast tomorrow."

George went to his room, realizing suddenly how very, very lonely his father was, sitting there night after night with no one to join him in front of the screen. He felt guilty for not spending more time with his father.

He felt more guilty as he lay on his bed looking up at the ceiling in the darkness and thinking of Professor Thompson. How unjust he had been to feel the Professor had any animosity toward him. The man had merely tried to help. The librarian, too. George had thought of her with suspicion, as if she were part of some conspiracy against him. What had been the matter with him?

He lay on his bed and wept.

For all his stupidity.

For Professor Thompson and the injustice he had done him.

For the girl in the library.

For Callum.

For all the misunderstood victims of circumstance the world around.

He sat up suddenly. Most of all, he felt a sadness for the

makers of Biskies. He had maligned them bitterly, although they knew nothing about it. He owed them an apology and wondered what he could do to make restitution. He could write a testimonial letter and offer some ideas for an advertising campaign. Something better, though — he might be able to find a way to remove the sawdust-and-molasses taste.

He went to sleep dreaming happily of ways to improve Biskies.

Sometime near morning George awoke with a horrible sickness in his bowels and in his head. His eyes felt as if they had been twisted around in their sockets.

His heart raced, and sweat bathed him in a cold, sticky layer.

He knew at once what was wrong. The metathorinate had been stronger than he had thought. He had to have more now. He craved it. He felt as if he could eat Biskies by the fistful to get at the metathorinate. If only he could get another spoonful of that sugar — but that was in his basement lab. He was too sick to go for it, and he couldn't ask any of his family.

And that was good. A spark of sanity told him he had to leave it alone. If he could get through the next few hours he would be all right. But another dose like the one he had taken last night would addict him to metathorinate forever. He had to have food.

His mother was solicitous but unnerved. She had never seen one of the children sick before. She didn't know what to do.

"Are you hungry?" she said.

He nodded weakly.

"Would you like some breakfast food? Some Biskies?"

He wanted to gulp it down by the bale. But he shook his head. "Go to the health food store. Get me something.

Anything. Get me some of their bread. And some synthmilk. Don't go anywhere else. That's the only food that will make me well."

He knew the risk in shopping at the health food store. It was allowed to exist and to proclaim the absence of additives and preservatives in its products. This gave the illusion of freedom. But its customers were carried on a special list. Their purchases were noted in the computer history.

"Hurry — please!" said George. Nausea racked him. He vomited all over the floor.

George's father was bewildered by such unusual circumstances, but he hurried out to the health food store. It was nineteen stories down. He hardly knew what to buy. He grabbed bread, synthmilk, some souplike concoctions, and sawdustlike breakfast food that looked just like Biskies but was called something else.

George stayed home that day, slowly recovering from the withdrawal of the potassium metathorinate. He recognized now how wrong he had been in supposing the chemical had no effect. It was slow, like a time bomb.

He pondered the effects of the chemical. It didn't work all by itself. The researchers who wrote of its dangers in the journal were right. There was a correlation between the distribution of the drug and TV work. The TV scripts were designed to induce a certain emotional state, but they were effective only if the viewer was under the influence of metathorinate.

This simple fact meant there was a vast coordination between the TV producers and the processors of bread, jam, vegetables, Biskies, and anything else preserved with the chemical.

Such coordination could come about in only one way: through government control. That meant the Government was responsible for the combined action of metathorinate and TV.

The idea was monstrous, incredible. Yet was it any more so than a thousand other aspects of the lives people led?

A century ago an ecology frenzy had swept the land. It had ended with controls so steel-fisted a man could not paint a chair in his own house without a permit from a bureau. Factories were choked out of existence until only government takeovers could keep them functioning — at vast increases in the prices of goods.

The Zero Population Growth fad — although it had come at a time when population was plummeting — had made parenthood a humiliation. This humiliation was still felt, even though there were now only fifty million people, where once there had been four times that number. And couples were still required to obtain a license to have children. Those born unlicensed were deprived of their full rights as citizens.

Surely a government able to impose these controls could also coordinate the food and entertainment industries to produce a given effect on the populace.

The more George thought about it, the more he realized it was consistent with the pattern of modern history which he had studied in school. Although the facts had been doctored to fit the approved historical concepts, they could not conceal the evidence of increasing strangulation of individual lives. This pattern had been set long ago, and there had been no deviation from it in more than a century.

He contemplated the TV show he had seen last night. Asinine in the extreme, it had held him and pummeled his emotions. The change it had produced in his thinking would have been permanent if he had had sufficient exposure to the combination of drug and screen.

The show had caused him to believe Professor Thompson was not part of the massive conspiracy, that the girl in the library was innocent of any opposition to him.

That was the greater thing. That was what it did for the thousands who watched it, doped with metathorinate. It

persuaded them that all the villains were good guys. There
was no evil. There was nothing to fight against. The world
was pure and shining, and animosity against anything and
anybody was a sinful thing.

The land had once been full of mobs and anger and
violence and dispute. He had read about it. Now there was
none. It had been cured — not by reason, not by agreement
and the healing of differences, but by illusion. A great,
hypnotic illusion that all was well and there were no enemies
anywhere. Peace had come to the land at last.

But George Williams had enemies.

He was sure Professor Thompson had noted on his record
that he had learned of the hallucinogenic characteristics of
potassium metathorinate. He had accused the library of
removing the journal, and the librarian would have entered
that in the record. And now it was recorded that his father
had made a purchase at the health food store.

Any one entry by itself would not be noticed. But the
computer would put them all together. The great bloodless
computer would signal some human lackey that George
Williams knew.

That he knew the enemy.

That he knew the massive conspiracy.

The enemy would move against him.

George was frightened. He was sick to his stomach. He
cried out in the night and had nightmares so terrible that he
was bathed in sweat when he awoke.

He stayed home from school another day. His sisters went
to school, and his parents went to work. They were all
growing disgusted with him. His father threatened to take
him to the Medical Floor. George knew he would be done
for if they ever got him there.

He forced himself to think more rationally and put the
panic aside during the day. He hadn't committed any overt

acts. Perhaps he was overestimating the degree of suppression they might use against him. Maybe if he didn't tip his hand any further they'd be content to watch him for a period. Surely that was logical.

He became more satisfied that his terrors had been exaggerated. By afternoon he was convinced that he could play it from here on without inviting trouble. He'd wait his time. There were escape routes. They were hardly accessible to a teenage boy, but he had only a few years to wait for maturity. Then he could escape this prison.

His father noticed the change in him that evening. "I'm glad you're feeling better, George. You looked like a scared dog this morning. What was the matter with you, anyway?"

"Something I ate. I'm all right now."

"Come and watch the shows with me tonight. I heard there's going to be something rather different. The story of a family in a city-building like ours, and a boy like you. He has some problems with the school and the authorities. It sounds interesting."

A tiny seed of terror burst somewhere inside him. "Sure, I'll watch it with you, Dad."

The boy's name was the same as his. George. Only they made the last name Walters instead of Williams. He, too, lived in a 130-story city-building, where schools and city services were located every twenty floors. In the reserve area in the basement of the building, George Walters raised small animals. Rabbits, mice, rats, pigeons.

Why did they bother to try to disguise him at all, George Williams wondered.

He sat with a knot in his belly and watched the screen. George Walters was a rebellious, disruptive boy. He believed his teachers in school were wrong about everything. He undermined their authority by talking to other students and showing them how wrong the teachers were. Many of the students became sullen and rebellious and failed in their school work. They were ultimately dismissed, their life careers ruined because of the agitation of George Walters. They finally recognized what harm he had done them and tried to get even with him.

George Walters believed that the government system of allocating professional positions was unfair. He wrote letters to heads of bureaus and directors of economic units. He believed he should have the right to go into a new business without a certificate of need and permission of the Bureau of Trade. He got several businessmen in trouble because they listened to him.

In the city-building he argued with the manager that he should have more space to raise larger animals. He wanted a horse. The manager, of course, penalized him by withdrawing some of the space he already had. George then went around with a petition to have the manager removed.

Turmoil and ill will crept through the entire city-building. People began taking sides and arguing with one another about the way George Walters was treated. They quarreled and even fought with one another when he was removed from school.

At the end of the show, the manager was pursuing George to punish him for stirring up the people of his building. There was a chase — a very exciting and breath-catching chase — through the building and up to the top level and out on the roof.

George slipped and fell from the very top of the building to a level fifty floors below. Hundreds of people saw his body drop past their windows.

On their faces were expressions of relief when they realized that the cause of all the turmoil was gone. The school authorities and the building manager and the bureau directors expressed sadness when they heard the news. Sadness that George Walters had made such a mess of his opportunities. And happiness that his influence was gone.

This was different from the Callum show. Callum had been shown to be a man of basic goodness, a victim of circumstance. The metathorinate-soaked brains of the audience accorded him forgiveness.

The same audience was shown no redeeming features in George Walters. They hated him. They exulted in his destruction. They would help destroy anything he represented.

They would destroy George Williams.

Somehow the panic, the fear, the sick sweatiness had receded. In its place was the simple agony of knowing every hand held a knife turned toward him. And he wondered, with some degree of amazement, how the show had been prepared so quickly. It had been written by computer, of course, after the machine had kicked out a red card on him. Even so, the production time must have been compressed enormously.

They weren't going to wait. They wanted him now.

"I liked that," said George's father. "Something different. I think that kid got what was coming to him, don't you?"

"Yes," said George. "I think he got what was coming to him."

He went to school the next day because there was nothing else to do.

On the escalators he heard them talking about the show. Everybody must have seen it. They all thought George Walters got what was coming to him.

"He did, didn't he?" Someone jibed and shouted in George's ear.

"Yeah, sure. He sure did," said George.

They started shoving, pummeling, fooling around. Somehow they all seemed to be pressing in on him. His case dropped and broke open, his books scattering.

He was down on the sharp steel steps of the escalator, and

they were trampling him. He struggled aside, grabbing at the legs and toppling three or four of those who kicked him. There were shrieks of insane laughter over his head. Then he saw what they had done.

Somehow they had loosened the cover at the top of the escalator. The steps were folding, disappearing into the grinding mechanism hidden under the floor. The opening seemed to speed toward him. As he struggled, a foot clamped on his neck.

He twisted furiously and grabbed at the leg that held him down. The form toppled, screamed. An arm was dragged into the gears and chains and torn off. The bloody figure was shoved up on the floor.

They scattered, yelling in fear and madness. He ran after them, glancing back only once at the figure that lay silently where George Williams had been meant to lie.

There was a hushed buzz in the classes that morning. The glances of all were upon George. It was clear, in the minds of everyone, that he was to blame for the accident that had happened to the other boy. He was avoided, not spoken to.

In the afternoon, in physics class, there was a demonstration of high-frequency electrical phenomena. The teacher exhibited a coil from which he drew two-foot sparks. Then, to demonstrate the harmlessness of such current at high voltage and low amperage, he asked George to come to the front.

"I want you to take hold of these two electrodes, George. It's not going to hurt. We're going to pass this current right through you and see how long a spark we can draw off the other end of this electrode. All right?"

George stepped forward and grasped the carbon handles. He glanced at the maze of wiring on the table and switchboard by the high-frequency coil. The instructor's hand moved toward the switch to connect the huge coil again.

George yelled involuntarily and dropped the electrodes, which clattered to the floor.

The class laughed in glee. The instructor laughed. "I hadn't even thrown the switch, George. What did you jump for?"

George pointed to the wiring on the table. "Those wires. You've got the electrodes connected directly to the low-voltage input. I would have been electrocuted!"

The instructor frowned and glanced down, following the wiring. He looked up with an amazed smile on his face. "Darned if you wouldn't, George. Darned if you wouldn't."

The class buckled with laughter.

He cornered his father after dinner. "I need to talk with you, Dad. I'm in trouble and I need some help."

His father glanced at the clock. "Sure, son. But I've got to watch the John and Angus show now. It's an hour and a half —"

George frightened himself with his own screams. "They're after me! Can't you understand that? They tried to kill me twice today, and they'll try again tomorrow. Isn't that more important to you than watching that — thing?"

He grasped a nearby bookend and hurled it at the screen. The shattering implosion sounded like a small bomb.

His father was white with anger. "You've destroyed the screen. It takes days to get it repaired. I guess you do need help." He turned to George's mother, who had hurried in with the two sisters at the sound of disaster. "Call the doctor at once before he destroys something else — or hurts one of us." He glared at his son's pleading face.

George's vision swam with tears. His father was like a mechanism. With the metathorinate and TV, his mind had not been his own for many years.

"You don't even know me, do you?" said George. "You don't even know me."

His mother and sisters stood frozen on the other side of the room.

The doctor hypo-shot him when he tried to run. "It's easier this way," the doctor said. "We don't have to struggle to hold them down any more. First used it on animals a long time ago. I don't know why they insisted for so long that a human patient had to be held down and injected directly instead of using one of these little bullet capsules. Anyway, get him on the bed and we'll take a look."

He put the little hypo pistol in his bag and waited impersonally while Mr. Williams wrestled his son to the bed.

George was conscious. He heard everything that was said and saw all that was done. He could even get up and walk if he wanted to. But he had no desire to walk or run or flee — not anymore. That was what they had done to him.

His father told the doctor how George had behaved. It had started only a few days ago when he had gotten sick after watching a show. Then he had come up with these hallucinations that somebody was trying to kill him, and had ended up by destroying the screen.

The doctor nodded sagely. "It's one of the problems we have to cope with in this tight environment we live in. Many years ago, when there was lots of open space for children to move around in, these symptoms were easily worked off and became harmless. Now we have a real problem.

"This sort of syndrome develops into a retrogressive disease that takes a person deep back into childhood. If we're early enough we may be able to halt the process. Special classes have been set up as part of the school system to deal with this problem. I'll make arrangements for you to enroll George at once."

George felt a surge of hope. Maybe they had changed their minds. Maybe they were just going to brainwash him. If that was what they intended, he would be the best student they ever had. He would convince them he believed all they said. He would tell them anything they wanted to hear. He would beat them yet. He would beat them yet. . . .

There were only eight other pupils in the class. He glanced warily at them, yet he felt an affinity for them. His own kind. There was a girl his own age on one side, and a boy maybe a year older on the other.

"I'm George Williams," he said.

The girl smiled. "I'm Vanessa Ipson. They call me Nessa."

The other boy said, "I'm Jim Farrington. Glad to know you."

They were different. Here for the same reason. "What're you in for?" he asked Nessa.

She glanced around, her face marked with sudden fear.

"I think we can talk to each other," said Jim Farrington. "We're all in the same situation. Nessa learned what they're doing with advertising. She discovered sublims in everything — TV, tapes, printed stuff. You can't escape it."

"It was outlawed decades ago," said Nessa. "But the Bureau of Economic Promotion actually requires a percentage of advertising to be sublim. They know there would be too many protests over its content, even in these times, if it were straight."

"I guess I don't know what sublims are," said George.

"Subliminal," said Nessa. "Communication below the level of consciousness. Quick flashes on the TV screen that aren't consciously observed, but you pick them up subconsciously. Patterns in printed advertising that the eye doesn't recognize, but a message is given to the brain. The same thing can be done aurally and even by touch and smell.

"Entrance into careers is controlled largely this way. Marriage and parenthood are, also. I don't know what else, but I think there must be a great many other things.

"This is utopia," the girl continued bitterly. "The goal of mankind through the ages. Ecological problems all solved. Population regulated so it can't get out of hand. No social dissent. A controlled level of income, determined by a computer, which will keep each person content within his natural limitations. Nobody thinks. Nobody steps out of line. They let a few frictions exist, a few personal problems — just enough to keep you thinking you are free."

"I found there is some kind of organization," said Jim. "It's so big that few of the members know anything of each other. They don't even understand fully the whole purpose of the thing. They communicate only by computer, and the computer filters all their communications according to a master pattern.

"Government is in it. Industry is in it. Entertainment is in it. The churches, the unions — every facet of society is part of it. It's a gigantic, self-perpetuating thing made possible by the computer. Without the computer, the system would never have grown to its present state. Without the computer, it would fall apart at once.

"But the computer allows the members to control each other just as, together, they control the population mass.

"Then, once in a while — because it is so big and pervasive that it can't be hidden completely — someone chips away a little corner of the cover that protects the system." He swept a hand about the room. "All of us here have done just that, in one way or another. And we've been caught. That's why we are here."

"What will they do to us?" asked George.

"They'll try to change our thinking. The secret is to agree with them in everything. We'll have our day. We've made mistakes by plunging too fast. Maybe we'll survive to have another chance."

Jim looked bitter. Nessa looked frightened. George no longer believed they had a chance. But he kept hoping.

The instructor arrived. He was a kindly-looking man with graying hair and a middle-aged face, but he spoke with youthful confidence and enthusiasm.

"I know every one of you is anxious to get back to your regular classes, and we're going to make that happen just as fast as we can." He paused and beamed over the small group. "Now, each of you knows what your own personal reason is for being here. You've had some misunderstandings concerning the functioning of important elements of our society and its relation to you as individuals. This is a special course to give you a broad understanding of those elements. Much of it is audio-visual. We will now begin, unless there are questions you'd like to ask first."

No one moved or spoke.

"I will step out of the room now and start the projection." The man smiled a final time and stepped through the door.

The room darkened and the screen lighted. There was some pat stuff about history, which seemed to have been lifted from class material George had already gone through. It didn't make sense. He glanced around. Nessa, Jim, and the others seemed to be wondering, too, what it was all about.

Then he became somehow aware of something new within the room. He couldn't feel it, but it was inside him. He couldn't see it, but it was in his eyes. It was in every cell of his being. He didn't know it by any physical sense, but he knew it was there. The room was filled with it from a hundred different sources, shooting in every direction to bathe every cell of their bodies, their genes, their chromosomes. Some kind of radiation.

He looked about in terror. He couldn't tell if the others felt it or not. "Jim — Nessa —" he whispered hoarsely.

"Yes — I feel it," said Jim. "I don't know what it's doing —"

Nessa began to cry softly.

He didn't know how long it was, but it seemed an eternity before the smiling, graying man returned. "There, now," he said. "I'm sure that helps you all to understand a little better. You won't be permitted to go home, of course, until the lessons are finished. You may now go to your quarters in the dormitory, however. You will be shown the way. . . ."

The progress of the course was measured by reading tests.

On the third day they were reading seventh-grade material.

On the fifth day they were reading fifth-grade material.

On the seventh day they were reading second-grade material.

They had breakfast together the next day in a small dining room. Nessa brought a brand-new doll someone had given her. She propped it against the table and tried to feed it some of the breakfast cereal. "Isn't she cute?" she asked the boys.

They nodded. They both liked Nessa. She didn't knock their blocks over when they had them stacked up, the way some of the other kids did.

George Williams picked up the cereal box. It looked so very familiar. He knew he had eaten this kind a lot of times, but he couldn't remember when. He picked out the words on the box, letter by letter.

Biskies.

A bowl of Biskies makes a growing boy.

It was the last thing he ever read.

In a world where robots and people work together, who will come out on top? The answer may surprise you.

THE NEW SEMESTER

DOUGLAS McLEOD

Theodore Goodman was nervous. Working strictly in the administrative branches of UniCom, he had never come in contact with the robots, and he was not quite sure how to handle them. Of course, he knew what he had read in the current status reports and was fully aware of the situation, but still, he had no way of knowing how the robot would react to what he was about to say — if it would react at all. One bothersome question after another turned over in his mind. Just how strong were these robots? Could they have developed some sort of self-preservation mechanism? And if they had —

The intercom's buzz pierced his thoughts.

"Mr. Goodman?" a hollow voice inquired.

"Yes?"

"R.I.-1 is here to see you."

"All right," he replied guardedly. "Send him in."

The door was flung open, and the machine walked stiffly into the office. It stopped abruptly inside the doorway, leveling its expressionless gaze on Goodman.

"Who are you?" it demanded immediately, with the usual lack of inflection in its voice.

Goodman managed a nervous smile. "Yes, I suppose you're wondering what's going on."

"Where is S-111?" the machine insisted.

Goodman looked baffled. "S-111? Oh, the robot who held this position before?" He paused. "I've replaced him," he said, then added, "temporarily, of course."

The robot seemed to accept this explanation. It closed the door, crossed the room and sat down in front of the desk.

"Now," Goodman began, "as to why you were called here." It was at just that moment that Goodman realized he didn't know what he was going to say. Well, that's not quite right. He knew what he was going to say, but he didn't know how he was going to say it. He hurriedly decided he should start at the roots of the problem — the Mechanized Education Program.

"The central computer probably has not made you aware of it [the central computer made the robots aware of as little as possible] but lately there has been quite a bit of dissatisfaction with the performance of our students." He picked up a dossier from the desk, inclined it toward the robot, then dropped it.

"Recent tests have shown a drop of almost two points in the average achievement/capability ratio. Interestingly enough, drops have also been noted in the average interest quotient, and of course, in such things as quarterly grades. Needless to say, the training director was very upset with all this. Slight declines can be anticipated, but nothing as drastic as we have experienced in the past semester."

Goodman paused, thinking he wasn't doing too badly so far, and watched the robot. It revealed nothing. The thing had not moved a mechanical muscle since he began, and no one could possibly read anything from those still, unblinking eyes. Oh, well.

"The directors," he continued, "have put a great deal of effort into tracking down the cause of the difficulty. In this case, there are only two possibilities. Either there is something wrong with the students, which is extremely doubtful, or —" he paused, eyeing the machine carefully, " — or, there is something wrong with the teachers."

The robot stirred millimetrically. Goodman noticed it, and it did not improve his composure a bit.

"Well," he went on, "assuming the latter was the case, the training director called an emergency board meeting. And at that meeting a very interesting idea was brought up." Here we go, Goodman thought, this is where you'll have to be very careful. "The idea, which has since been put into operation, is to replace all robot-teachers with humans."

This time the machine's movements were far from millimetric. It suddenly sat forward in its chair, and its eyes almost seemed to be glaring now. "That would not be a wise idea," it advised immediately.

"Well, let me finish," Goodman said, not as firmly as he could have. "Naturally, the directors would not start a program of this size without some very good reasons." He sorted out all the very good reasons in his mind. "From the results of the achievement/capability tests, it is clear that the robot-teachers are doing something wrong. I believe the sudden decline in the interest quotient indicates just what it is — the robots have failed to interest the students in their particular subject."

"That argument was defeated when the Mechanized Education Program was first instituted," the machine stated evenly.

"Yes, I know," Goodman conceded. "But obviously, that decision was a wrong one, or the a/c scores would be two points higher. In any case, some very basic ideas support this theory." Goodman decided that since he was dealing with a logical mind, it would be best to present the argument as logically as possible.

"In order to be really effective," he explained, "a teacher must create interest in the subject he is teaching. If he fails to do this, the student does not learn everything he is capable of learning. To create this interest, the teacher must himself show interest. Well," Goodman said matter-of-factly, "robots cannot show interest, or any other human quality for that matter. Because they cannot show it, they cannot create it, and therefore —" he pointed to the dossier on his desk, " — the decline in a/c scores." He leaned back in the chair, giving the machine a little time to let this sink in. It did not take long.

"Interest is not a relevant factor," the robot stated, almost with finality.

"But it is," Goodman insisted. "In humans. You see, there is a great deal of difference between being taught and actually learning. Being taught requires relatively little, but to learn, there must be interest."

"Non sequitur," the robot intoned. "Interest is not relevant."

Goodman exhaled loudly. "Well," he said, "like it or not, you can't fight it."

The robot clearly intended to try. It stood up, shoving the chair back with so much force it almost fell over. "In addition to the obvious fallacy on which your idea is based," it began, "there are several points which make it impractical."

Goodman may have been imagining it, but the machine's voice seemed to be getting louder.

"First. To put this plan into operation, it would be necessary to employ hundreds of humans who are presently engaged in more important positions."

"That's partially true," Goodman admitted. "We would have to employ hundreds of humans, but not necessarily from more important positions. I consider this job as important as any they could be holding now."

The robot did not bother to reply. "Second," it announced, walking stiffly around the desk and glaring down at Goodman. "Financial reasons."

Goodman was becoming increasingly nervous. There was now nothing between himself and the machine, and he had not been mistaken — its voice was getting louder.

"The yearly cost of such an operation would be enormous. Approximately —" it paused momentarily, staring blankly

off into space, then switched its gaze back to Goodman, " —
approximately $5,000,271,325."

"Yes, yes, I'm aware of all that," Goodman said nervously.
"And so are the directors. They have planned it all out very
carefully." He started to get up, but a vise-like metal hand
clamped onto his shoulder and shoved him back down into
the chair. Goodman massaged his sore shoulder gently,
silently cursing the machine.

"Third," it droned loudly as it walked back around the
desk. "Effect on the students. The sudden appearance of
human teachers would cause great distraction among the
students, and their performance would suffer as a result.
Then after the initial shock wore off, there would remain
minor irritants such as the tendency for voice fluctuation.
This would cause a serious concentration problem."

Goodman probably would have found that amusing, but
the robot's voice, booming now in the small confines of the
office, was just short of causing physical pain. He heaved
himself out of the chair and held up his hands.

"I'm sorry," he interrupted, "but there's no use arguing.
There is nothing you can do about it now. The decision has
been made, and it's final."

The machine slammed a gleaming fist on the desktop.
"No!" it boomed. "You may not replace me!" A chromium
steel arm shot across the desk and tried to grab Goodman.
The move took him completely by surprise, but he managed
to reel back in time, so that all the robot got was the lapel
off his coat. The machine threw the tattered piece of cloth to
the floor and stalked menacingly around the end of the desk.
Goodman threw open a drawer, fumbling desperately for the
only thing that could protect him. He got a grip on it, whirled
around, and pressed the button. The machine stopped dead
in its tracks not three feet away, its arms outstretched as if
to seize him. It swayed delicately for a second or two, then
keeled over forward, hitting the floor with a resounding,

reassuring crash. Goodman collapsed in his chair and sat there for several moments, breathing heavily, and waiting for his pulse to return to a normal rate. He then picked up the inanimate robot, dragged it across the room, and dumped it unceremoniously in the closet. He wanted to change his suit, but he did not have time. He just took off his jacket and threw it in on top of the machine. He walked back to his desk, straightened his tie and picked up the deactivating unit, this time putting it in his pocket.

The intercom buzzed.

"Mr. Goodman?" the hollow voice inquired.

"Yes?"

"R.I.-2 is here to see you."

"All right," Goodman replied, still panting a little. "Send him in."

Charley's just an ordinary guy. He's been in and out of Grand Central Station hundreds of times, and he knows there are only two levels there. So when he thinks he has found a third level, he must be losing his mind. Right? Read on.

THE THIRD LEVEL

JACK FINNEY

The presidents of the New York Central and the New York, New Haven and Hartford railroads will swear on a stack of timetables that there are only two. But I say there are three, because I've *been* on the third level at Grand Central Station. Yes, I've taken the obvious step: I talked to a psychiatrist friend of mine, among others. I told him about the third level at Grand Central Station, and he said it was a waking-dream wish fulfillment. He said I was unhappy. That made my wife kind of mad, but he explained that he meant the modern world is full of insecurity, fear, war, worry, and all the rest of it, and that I just want to escape. Well, hell, who doesn't? Everybody I know wants to escape, but they don't wander down into any third level at Grand Central Station.

But that's the reason, he said, and my friends all agreed. Everything points to it, they claimed. My stamp-collecting, for example — that's a "temporary refuge from reality." Well, maybe, but my grandfather didn't need any refuge from reality; things were pretty nice and peaceful in his day, from all I hear, and he started my collection. It's a nice collection, too, blocks of four of practically every U.S. issue, first-day covers, and so on. President Roosevelt collected stamps, too, you know.

Anyway, here's what happened at Grand Central. One night last summer I worked late at the office. I was in a hurry to get uptown to my apartment, so I decided to subway from Grand Central because it's faster than the bus.

Now, I don't know why this should have happened to me. I'm just an ordinary guy named Charley, thirty-one years old, and I was wearing a tan gabardine suit and a straw hat with a fancy band — I passed a dozen men who looked just like me. And I wasn't trying to escape from anything; I just wanted to get home to Louisa, my wife.

I turned into Grand Central from Vanderbilt Avenue and went down the steps to the first level, where you take trains like the Twentieth Century. Then I walked down another flight to the second level, where the suburban trains leave from, ducked into an arched doorway heading for the subway — and got lost. That's easy to do. I've been in and out of Grand Central hundreds of times, but I'm always bumping into new doorways and stairs and corridors. Once I got into a tunnel about a mile long and came out in the lobby of the Roosevelt Hotel. Another time I came up in an office building on Forty-sixth Street, three blocks away.

Sometimes I think Grand Central is growing like a tree, pushing out new corridors and staircases like roots. There's probably a long tunnel that nobody knows about feeling its way under the city right now, on its way to Times Square, and maybe another to Central Park. And maybe — because for so many people through the years Grand Central *has* been an exit, a way of escape — maybe that's how the tunnel I got into . . . but I never told my psychiatrist friend about that idea.

The corridor I was in began angling left and slanting downward and I thought that was wrong, but I kept on walking. All I could hear was the empty sound of my own footsteps and I didn't pass a soul. Then I heard that sort of hollow roar ahead that means open space, and people talking. The tunnel turned sharp left; I went down a short flight of stairs and came out on the third level at Grand Central Station. For just a moment I thought I was back on the second level, but I saw the room was smaller, there were fewer ticket windows and train gates, and the information booth in the center was wood and old-looking. And the man in the booth wore a green eyeshade and long, black sleeve-protectors. The lights were dim and sort of flickering. Then I saw why; they were open-flame gaslights.

There were brass spittoons on the floor, and across the station a glint of light caught my eye; a man was pulling a gold watch from his vest pocket. He snapped open the cover, glanced at his watch, and frowned. He wore a dirty hat, a black four-button suit with tiny lapels, and he had a big, black handlebar mustache. Then I looked around and saw that everyone in the station was dressed like 1890 something; I never saw so many beards, sideburns and fancy mustaches in my life. A woman walked in through the train gate; she wore a dress with leg-of-mutton sleeves and skirts to the top of her high-buttoned shoes. Back of her, out on the tracks, I caught a glimpse of a locomotive, a very small Currier & Ives locomotive with a funnel-shaped stack. And then I knew.

To make sure, I walked over to a newsboy and glanced at the stack of papers at his feet. It was the *World*, and the *World* hasn't been published for years. The lead story said something about President Cleveland. I've found that front page since, in the Public Library files, and it was printed June 11, 1894.

I turned toward the ticket windows knowing that here — on the third level at Grand Central — I could buy tickets that would take Louisa and me anywhere in the United States we wanted to go. In the year 1894. And I wanted two tickets to Galesburg, Illinois.

Have you ever been there? It's a wonderful town still, with big old frame houses, huge lawns, and tremendous trees whose branches meet overhead and roof the streets. And in 1894, summer evenings were twice as long, and people sat out on their lawns, the men smoking cigars and talking quietly, the women waving palm-leaf fans, with the fireflies all around, in a peaceful world. To be back there with the first World War still 20 years off, and World War II over 40 years in the future . . . I wanted two tickets for that.

The clerk figured the fare — he glanced at my fancy hatband, but he figured the fare — and I had enough for two coach tickets, one way. But when I counted out the money and looked up, the clerk was staring at me. He nodded at the bills. "That ain't money, mister," he said, "and if you're trying to skin me you won't get very far," and he glanced at the cash drawer beside him. Of course the money was old-style bills, half again as big as the money we use nowadays, and different-looking. I turned away and got out fast. There's nothing nice about jail, even in 1894.

And that was that. I left the same way I came, I suppose. Next day, during lunch hour, I drew $300 out of the bank, nearly all we had, and bought old-style currency (that *really* worried my psychiatrist friend). You can buy old money at almost any coin dealer's, but you have to pay a premium. My $300 bought less than $200 in old-style bills, but I didn't care; eggs were thirteen cents a dozen in 1894.

But I've never again found the corridor that leads to the third level at Grand Central Station, although I've tried often enough.

Louisa was pretty worried when I told her all this and didn't want me to look for the third level anymore, and after a while I stopped; I went back to my stamps. But now we're *both* looking, every weekend, because now we have proof that the third level is still there. My friend Sam Weiner disappeared! Nobody knew where, but I sort of suspected because Sam's a city boy, and I used to tell him about Galesburg — I went to school there — and he always said he liked the sound of the place. And that's where he is, all right. In 1894.

Because one night, fussing with my stamp collection, I found — Well, do you know what a first-day cover is? When a new stamp is issued, stamp collectors buy some and use them to mail envelopes to themselves on the very first day of sale; and the postmark proves the date. The envelope is called a first-day cover. They're never opened; you just put blank paper in the envelope.

That night, among my oldest first-day covers, I found one that shouldn't have been there. But there it was. It was there because someone had mailed it to my grandfather at his home in Galesburg; that's what the address on the envelope said. And it had been there since July 18, 1894 — the postmark showed that — yet I didn't remember it at all. The stamp was a six-cent, dull brown, with a picture of President Garfield. Naturally, when the envelope came to Granddad in the mail, it went right into his collection and stayed there — till I took it out and opened it.

The paper inside wasn't blank. It read:

> 941 Willard Street
> Galesburg, Illinois
> July 18, 1894

Charley:

I got to wishing that you were right. Then I got to *believing* you were right. And, Charley, it's true; I found the third level! I've been here two weeks, and right now, down the street at the Dalys', someone is playing a piano, and they're all out on the front porch singing *Seeing Nellie Home*. And I'm invited over for lemonade. Come on back, Charley and Louisa. Keep looking till you find the third level! It's worth it, believe me!

The note is signed Sam.

At the stamp and coin store I go to, I found out that Sam bought $800 worth of old-style currency. That ought to set him up in a nice little hay, feed, and grain business; he always said that's what he really wished he could do, and he certainly can't go back to his old business. Not in Galesburg, Illinois, in 1894. His old business? Why, Sam was my psychiatrist.

Cadet Michael Farthingworth has a big problem. He's accident prone — well, more like catastrophe prone. His superiors are ready to give up. Can anyone solve Michael's problem?

PRONE

MACK REYNOLDS

SupCom Bull Underwood said in a voice ominously mild, "I continually get the impression that every other sentence is being left out of this conversation. Now, tell me, General, what do you mean *things happen around him?*"

"Well, for instance, the first day Mitchie got to the Academy a cannon burst at a demonstration."

"What's a cannon?"

"A pre-guided-missile weapon," the commander of the Terra Military Academy told him. "You know, shells propelled by gunpowder. We usually demonstrate them in our history classes. This time four students were injured. The next day sixteen were hurt in ground-war maneuvers."

There was an element of respect in the SupCom's tone. "Your course must be rugged."

General Bentley wiped his forehead with a snowy handkerchief even as he shook it negatively. "It was the first time any such thing happened. I tell you, sir, since Mitchie Farthingworth has been at the academy, things have been chaotic. Fires in the dormitories, small arms exploding, cadets being hospitalized right and left. We've just got to expel that boy!"

"Don't be ridiculous," the SupCom growled. "He's the apple of his old man's eye. We've got to make a hero out of him if it means the loss of a battle fleet. But I still don't get this. You mean the Farthingworth kid is committing sabotage?"

"It's not that. We investigated. He doesn't do it on purpose, things just *happen* around him. Mitchie can't help it."

"Confound it, stop calling him Mitchie!" Bull Underwood snapped. "How do you know it's him if he doesn't do it? Maybe you're just having a run of bad luck."

"That's what I thought," Bentley said, "until I ran into Admiral Lawrence of the Space Marines Academy. He had the same story. The day Mitchie — excuse me, sir — Michael Farthingworth set foot in Nuevo San Diego, things started happening. When they finally got him transferred to our academy the trouble stopped."

It was at times like these that Bull Underwood regretted his shaven head. He could have used some hair to tear. "Then it *must* be sabotage if it stops when he leaves!"

"I don't think so, sir."

The SupCom took a deep breath, snapped to his secretarobot, "Brief me on Cadet Michael Farthingworth, including his early life." While he waited he growled under his breath, "A stalemated hundred-year war on my hands with those Martian *makrons* and I have to get things like this tossed at me."

In less than a minute the secretarobot began: "Son of Senator Warren Farthingworth, Chairman War Appropriations Committee. Twenty-two years of age. Five feet six, one hundred and thirty, blue eyes, brown hair, fair. Born and spent early youth in former United States area. Early education by mother. At age of eighteen entered Harvard but schooling was interrupted when roof of assembly hall collapsed killing most of faculty. Next year entered Yale, leaving two months after when 90 percent of the university's buildings were burnt down in the holocaust of '85. Next attended University of California but failed to graduate owing to the earthquake which completely . . . "

"That's enough," the SupCom rapped. He turned and

stared at General Bentley. "What is it? Even if the kid was a psychokinetic saboteur he couldn't accomplish all that."

The academy commander shook his head. "All I know is that, since his arrival at the Terra Military Academy, there's been an endless series of casualties. And the longer he's there the worse it gets. It's twice as bad now as when he first arrived." He got to his feet wearily. "I'm a broken man, sir, and I'm leaving this in your hands. You'll have my resignation this afternoon. Frankly, I'm afraid to return to the school. If I do, some day I'll probably crack my spine bending over to tie my shoelaces. It just isn't safe to be near that boy."

For a long time after General Bentley had left, SupCom Bull Underwood sat at his desk, his heavy underlip in a pout. "And just when the next five years' appropriation is up before the committee," he snarled at nobody.

He turned to the secretarobot. "Put the best psychotechnicians available on Michael Farthingworth. They are to discover . . . well, they are to discover why things happen around him. Priority one."

Approximately a week later the secretarobot said, "May I interrupt you, sir? A priority-one report is coming in."

Bull Underwood grunted and turned away from the star chart he'd been studying with the two Space Marine generals. He dismissed them and sat down at his desk.

The visor lit up and he was confronted with the face of an elderly civilian. "Doctor Duclos," the civilian said. "Case of Cadet Michael Farthingworth."

"Good," the SupCom rumbled. "Doctor, what in the devil is wrong with young Farthingworth?"

"The boy is an accident prone."

Bull Underwood scowled at him. "A what?"

"An accident prone." The doctor elaborated with evident satisfaction. "There is indication that he is the most extreme case in medical history. Really, a fascinating study. Never in my experience have I been —"

"Please, Doctor. I'm a layman. What is an accident prone?"

"Ah, yes. Briefly, an unexplained phenomenon first noted by the insurance companies of the nineteenth and twentieth centuries. An accident prone has an unnaturally large number of accidents happen either to him, or less often, to persons in his vicinity. In Farthingworth's case, they happen to persons about him. He himself is never affected."

The SupCom was unbelieving. "You mean to tell me there are some persons who just naturally have accidents happen to them without any reason?"

"That is correct," Duclos nodded. "Most prones are understandable. Subconsciously, the death wish is at work and the prone *seeks* self-destruction. However, science has yet to discover the forces behind the less common type such as Farthingworth exemplifies." The doctor's emphatic shrug betrayed his Gallic background. "It has been suggested that it is no more than the laws of chance at work. To counterbalance the accident prone, there should be persons at the other extreme who are blessed with abnormally good fortune. However . . . "

SupCom Bull Underwood's lower lip was out, almost truculently. "Listen," he interrupted. "What can be done about it?"

"Nothing," the doctor said, his shoulders raising and lowering again. "An accident prone seems to remain one as a rule. Not always, but as a rule. Fortunately, they are rare."

"Not rare enough," the SupCom growled. "These insurance companies, what did they do when they located an accident prone?"

"They kept track of him and refused to insure the prone, his business, home, employees, employers, or anyone or anything connected with him."

Bull Underwood stared unblinkingly at the doctor, as though wondering whether the other's whole explanation was an attempt to pull his leg. Finally he rapped, "Thank you, Doctor Duclos. That will be all." The civilian's face faded from the visor.

The SupCom said slowly to the secretarobot, "Have Cadet Farthingworth report to me." He added *sotto voce*, "And while he's here have all personnel keep their fingers crossed."

The photoelectric-controlled door leading to the sanctum sanctorum of SupCom Bull Underwood glided quietly open and a lieutenant entered and came to a snappy attention. The door swung gently shut behind him.

"Well?" Bull Underwood growled.

"Sir, a Cadet Michael Farthingworth to report to you."

"Send him in. Ah, just a minute, Lieutenant Brown. How do you feel after talking to him?"

"Me, sir? I feel fine, sir." The lieutenant looked blankly at him.

"Hmmm. Well, send him in, confound it."

The lieutenant turned and the door opened automatically before him. "Cadet Farthingworth," he announced.

The newcomer entered and stood stiffly before the desk of Earth's military head. Bull Underwood appraised him with care. In spite of the swank Academy uniform, Michael Farthingworh cut a wistfully ineffectual figure. His faded blue eyes blinked sadly behind heavy contact lenses.

"That'll be all, Lieutenant," the SupCom said to his aide.

"Yes, sir." The lieutenant about-faced snappily and marched to the door — which swung sharply forward and quickly back again before the lieutenant was halfway through.

SupCom Bull Underwood winced at the crush of bone and cartilage. He shuddered, then snapped to his secretarobot, "Have Lieutenant Brown hospitalized . . . and, ah . . . see he gets a Luna Medal for exposing himself to danger beyond the call of duty."

He swung to the newcomer and came directly to the point. "Cadet Farthingworth," he rapped, "do you know what an accident prone is?"

Mitchie's voice was low and plaintive. "Yes, sir."

"You do?" Bull Underwood was surprised.

"Yes, sir. At first such things as the school's burning down didn't particularly impress me as being personally connected with me, but the older I get, the worse it gets, and after what happened to my first date, I started to investigate."

The SupCom said cautiously, "What happened to the date?"

Mitchie flushed. "I took her to a dance and she broke her leg."

The SupCom cleared his throat. "So finally you investigated?"

"Yes, sir," Mitchie Farthingworth said woefully. "And I found I was an accident prone and getting worse geometrically. Each year I'm twice as bad as the year before. I'm glad you've discovered it too, sir. I . . . didn't know what to do. Now it's in your hands."

The SupCom was somewhat relieved. Possibly this wasn't going to be as difficult as he had feared. He said, "Have you any ideas, Mitchie, ah, that is . . . "

"Call me Mitchie if you want, sir. Everybody else does."

"Have you any ideas? After all, you've done as much damage to Terra as a Martian task force would accomplish."

"Yes, sir. I think I ought to be shot."

"Huh?"

"Yes, sir. I'm expendable," Mitchie said miserably. "In fact, I suppose I'm probably the most expendable soldier that's ever been. All my life I've wanted to be a spaceman and do my share toward licking the Martians." His eyes gleamed behind his lenses. "Why, I've . . . "

He stopped and looked at his commanding officer pathetically. "What's the use? I'm just a bust. An accident prone.

The only thing to do is liquidate me." He tried to laugh in self-deprecation but his voice broke.

Behind him, Bull Underwood heard the glass in his office window shatter without seeming cause. He winced again, but didn't turn.

"Sorry, sir," Mitchie said. "See? The only thing is to shoot me."

"Look," Bull Underwood said urgently, "stand back a few yards farther, will you? There on the other side of the room." He cleared his throat. "Your suggestion has already been considered, as a matter of fact. However, due to your father's political prominence, shooting you had to be ruled out."

From a clear sky the secretarobot began to say, "'Twas brillig, and the slithy toves did gyre and gimble in the wabe."

SupCom Bull Underwood closed his eyes in pain and shrank back into his chair. "What?" he said cautiously.

"The borogoves were mimsy as all get-out," the secretarobot said decisively and shut up.

Mitchie looked at it. "Slipped its cogs, sir," he said helpfully. "It's happened before around me."

"The best memory bank in the system," Underwood protested. "Oh, no."

"Yes, sir," Mitchie said apologetically, "And I wouldn't recommend trying to repair it, sir. Three technicians were electrocuted when I was . . . "

The secretarobot sang, "O frabjous day! Callooh! Callay!"

"Completely around the corner," Mitchie said.

"This," said Bull Underwood, "is too frabjous much! Senator or no Senator, appropriations or no appropriations, with my own bare hands —"

As he strode impulsively forward, he felt the rug giving way beneath him. He grasped desperately for the edge of the desk, felt ink bottle and water carafe go crashing over.

Mitchie darted forward to his assistance.

"Stand back!" Bull Underwood roared, holding an ankle

with one hand, shaking the other hand in the form of a fist. "Get out of here, confound it!" Ink began to drip from the desk over his shaven head. It cooled him not at all. "It's not even safe to destroy you! It'd wipe out a regiment to try to assemble a firing squad! It — " Suddenly he paused, and when he spoke again his voice was like the coo of a condor.

"Cadet Farthingworth," he announced, "after considerable deliberation on my part I have chosen you to perform the most hazardous operation that Terra's forces have undertaken in the past hundred years. If successful, this effort will undoubtedly end the war."

"Who, me?" Mitchie said.

"Exactly," SupCom Underwood snapped. "This war has been going on for a century without either side's being able to secure that slight edge, that minute advantage which would mean victory. Cadet Farthingworth, you have been chosen to make the supreme effort which will give Terra that superiority over the Martians." The SupCom looked sternly at Mitchie.

"Yes, sir," he clipped. "What are my orders?"

The SupCom beamed at him. "Spoken like a true hero of Terra's Space Forces. On the spaceport behind this building is a small spycraft. You are to repair immediately to it and blast off for Mars. Once there, you are to land, hide the ship, and make your way to their capital city."

"Yes, sir! And what do I do then?"

"Nothing," Bull Underwood said with satisfaction. "You do absolutely nothing but live there. I estimate that your presence in the enemy capital will end the war in less than two years."

Michael Farthingworth snapped him a brilliant salute. "Yes, sir."

Spontaneous combustion broke out in the wastebasket.

Through the shards of his window, SupCom Bull Underwood could hear the blast-off of the spyship. Half a dozen miles away the flare of a fuel dump going up in flames lighted up the sky.

Seated there in the wreckage of his office he rubbed his ankle tenderly. "The only trouble is when the war is over we'll have to bring him home."

But then he brightened. "Perhaps we could leave him there as our occupation forces. It would keep them from ever recovering to the point where they could try again."

He tried to get to his feet, saying to the secretarobot, "Have them send me in a couple of medical corpsmen."

"Beware the Jabberwock," the secretarobot sneered.

This story by Arthur C. Clarke is a mystery — with a twist.

TROUBLE WITH TIME

ARTHUR C. CLARKE

"We don't have much crime on Mars," said Detective Inspector Rawlings, a little sadly. "In fact, that's the chief reason I'm going back to the Yard. If I stayed here much longer, I'd get completely out of practice."

We were sitting in the main observation lounge of the Phobos Spaceport, looking out across the jagged, sun-drenched crags of the tiny moon. The ferry rocket that had brought us up from Mars had left ten minutes ago, and was now beginning the long fall back to the ocher-tinted globe hanging there against the stars. In half an hour we would be boarding the liner for Earth — a world upon which most of the passengers had never set foot, but which they still called "home."

"At the same time," continued the Inspector, "now and then there's a case that makes life interesting. You're an art dealer, Mr. Maccar; I'm sure you heard about that spot of bother at Meridian City a couple of months ago."

"I don't think so," replied the plump, olive-skinned little man I'd taken for just another returning tourist. Presumably the Inspector had already checked through the passenger list; I wondered how much he knew about me, and tried to reassure myself that my conscience was — well — reasonably clear. After all, everybody took *something* out through Martian Customs —

"It's been rather well hushed up," said the Inspector, "but you can't keep these things quiet for long. Anyway, a jewel thief from Earth tried to steal Meridian Museum's greatest treasure — the Siren Goddess."

"But that's absurd!" I objected. "It's priceless, of course — but it's only a lump of sandstone. You couldn't sell it to anyone — you might just as well steal the Mona Lisa."

The Inspector grinned, rather mirthlessly. "*That's* happened once," he said. "Maybe the motive was the same. There are collectors who would give a fortune for such an object, even if they could only look at it themselves. Don't you agree, Mr. Maccar?"

"That's perfectly true. In my business, you meet all sorts of crazy people."

"Well, this chappie — name's Danny Weaver — had been well paid by one of them. And if it hadn't been for a piece of fantastically bad luck, he might have brought it off."

The Spaceport P.A. system apologized for a further slight delay owing to final fuel checks, and asked a number of passengers to report to Information. While we were waiting for the announcement to finish, I recalled what little I knew about the Siren Goddess. Though I'd never seen the original, like most other departing tourists I had a replica in my baggage. It bore the certificate of the Mars Bureau of Antiquities, guaranteeing that "this full-scale reproduction is an exact copy of the so-called Siren Goddess, discovered in the Mare Sirenium by the Third Expedition, A.D. 2012 (A.M. 23)."

It's quite a tiny thing to have caused so much controversy. Only eight or nine inches high — you wouldn't look at it twice if you saw it in a museum on Earth. The head of a young woman, with slightly Oriental features, elongated earlobes, hair curled in tight ringlets close to the scalp, lips half parted in an expression of pleasure or surprise — that's all. But it's an enigma so baffling that it's inspired a hundred religious sects, and driven quite a few archaeologists round the bend. For a perfectly human head has no right whatsoever to be found on Mars, whose only intelligent inhabitants were crustaceans — "educated lobsters," as the newspapers are fond of calling them. The aboriginal Martians never came near to achieving space flight, and in any event their civilization died before men existed on Earth. No wonder the Goddess is the solar system's number-one mystery; I don't suppose we'll find the answer in my lifetime — if we ever do.

"Danny's plan was beautifully simple," continued the Inspector. "You know how absolutely dead a Martian city gets on Sunday, when everything closes down and the colonists stay home to watch the TV from Earth. Danny was counting on this, when he checked into the hotel in Meridian West, late Friday afternoon. He'd have Saturday for reconnoitering the Museum, an undisturbed Sunday for the job itself, and on Monday morning he'd be just another tourist leaving town. . . .

"Early Saturday he strolled through the little park and crossed over into Meridian East, where the Museum stands. In case you don't know, the city gets its name because it's exactly on longitude one hundred and eighty degrees; there's a big stone slab in the park with the prime meridian engraved on it, so that visitors can get themselves photographed standing in two hemispheres at once. Amazing what simple things amuse some people.

"Danny spent the day going over the Museum, exactly like any other tourist determined to get his money's worth. But at closing time he didn't leave; he'd holed up in one of the galleries not open to the public, where the Museum had been arranging a Late Canal Period reconstruction but had run out of money before the job could be finished. He stayed there until about midnight, just in case there were any enthusiastic researchers still in the building. Then he emerged and got to work."

"Just a minute," I interrupted. "What about the night watchman?"

The Inspector laughed.

"My dear chap! They don't have such luxuries on Mars. There weren't even any alarms, for who would bother to steal lumps of stone? True, the Goddess was sealed up neatly in a strong glass-and-metal cabinet, just in case some souvenir hunter took a fancy to her. But even if she were stolen, there was nowhere the thief could hide, and of course all outgoing traffic would be searched as soon as the statue was missed."

That was true enough. I'd been thinking in terms of Earth, forgetting that every city on Mars is a closed little world of its own beneath the force-field that protects it from the freezing near-vacuum. Beyond those electronic shields is the utterly hostile emptiness of the Martian Outback, where a man will die in seconds without protection. That makes law enforcement very easy; no wonder there's so little crime on Mars. . . .

"Danny had a beautiful set of tools, as specialized as a watchmaker's. The main item was a microsaw no bigger than a soldering iron; it had a wafer-thin blade, driven at a million cycles a second by an ultrasonic power pack. It would go through glass or metal like butter — and left a cut only about as thick as a hair. Which was very important for Danny, since he had to leave no traces of his handiwork.

"I suppose you've guessed how he intended to operate. He was going to cut through the base of the cabinet, and substitute one of those souvenir replicas for the real Goddess. It might be a couple of years before some inquisitive expert discovered the awful truth; long before then the original would have traveled back to Earth, perfectly disguised as a copy of itself, with a genuine certificate of authenticity. Pretty neat, eh?

"It must have been a weird business, working in that darkened gallery with all those million-year-old carvings and unexplainable artifacts around him. A museum on Earth is bad enough at night, but at least it's — well — *human*. And

Gallery Three, which houses the Goddess, is particularly unsettling. It's full of bas-reliefs showing quite incredible animals fighting each other; they look rather like giant beetles, and most paleontologists flatly deny that they could ever have existed. But imaginary or not, they belonged to this world, and they didn't disturb Danny as much as the Goddess, staring at him across the ages and defying him to explain her presence here. She gave him the creeps. How do I know? He told me.

"Danny set to work on that cabinet as carefully as any diamond cutter preparing to cleave a gem. It took most of the night to slice out the trap door, and it was nearly dawn when he relaxed and put down the saw. There was still a lot of work to do, but the hardest part was over. Putting the replica into the case, checking its appearance against the photos he'd thoughtfully brought with him, and covering up his traces might take most of Sunday, but that didn't worry him in the least. He had another twenty-four hours, and would positively welcome Monday's first visitors so that he could mingle with them and make his inconspicuous exit.

"It was a perfectly horrible shock to his nervous system, therefore, when the main doors were noisily unbarred at eight-thirty and the museum staff — all six of them — started to open up for the day. Danny bolted for the emergency exit, leaving everything behind — tools, Goddesses, the lot. He had another big surprise when he found himself in the street; it should have been completely deserted at this time of day, with everyone at home reading the Sunday papers. But here were the citizens of Meridian East, as large as life, heading for plant or office on what was obviously a normal working day.

"By the time poor Danny got back to his hotel, we were waiting for him. We couldn't claim much credit for deducing that only a visitor from Earth — and a very recent one at that — could have overlooked Meridian City's chief claim to fame. And I presume you know what *that* is."

"Frankly, I don't," I answered. "You can't see much of Mars in six weeks, and I never went east of the Syrtis Major."

"Well, it's absurdly simple, but we shouldn't be too hard on Danny; even the locals occasionally fall into the same trap. It's something that doesn't bother us on Earth, where we've been able to dump the problem in the Pacific Ocean. But Mars, of course, is all dry land; and that means that *somebody* has to live with the International Date Line. . . .

"Danny, you see, had worked from Meridian West. It was Sunday over there all right — and it was still Sunday when we picked him up back at the hotel. But over in Meridian East, half a mile away, it was only Saturday. That little trip across the park had made all the difference; I told you it was rotten luck."

There was a long moment of silent sympathy; then I asked, "What did he get?"

"Three years," said Inspector Rawlings.

"That doesn't seem very much."

"Mars years; that makes it almost six of ours. And a whacking fine which, by an odd coincidence, came to just the refund value of his return ticket to Earth. He isn't in jail, of course; Mars can't afford that kind of nonproductive luxury. Danny has to work for a living, under discreet surveillance. I told you that the Meridian Museum couldn't afford a night watchman. Well, it has one now. Guess who."

"All passengers prepare to board in ten minutes! Please collect your hand baggage!" ordered the loud-speakers.

As we started to move toward the air lock, I couldn't help asking one more question.

"What about the people who put Danny up to it? There must have been a lot of money behind him. Did you get them?"

"Not yet; they'd covered their tracks pretty thoroughly, and I believe Danny was telling the truth when he said he couldn't give us any leads. Still, it's not my case; as I told you, I'm going back to my old job at the Yard. But a policeman always keeps his eyes open — like an art dealer, eh, Mr. Maccar? Why, you look a bit green about the gills. Have one of my space-sickness tablets."

"No, thank you," answered Mr. Maccar, "I'm quite all right."

His tone was distinctly unfriendly; the social temperature seemed to have dropped below zero in the last few minutes. I looked at Mr. Maccar, and I looked at the Inspector. And suddenly I realized that we were going to have a very interesting trip.

Kent Fowler has sent four men to Jupiter, and none of them have returned. He can't bear to send another man. But he knows that's the only sure way to find out what happened to the others.

DESERTION

CLIFFORD D. SIMAK

Four men, two by two, had gone into the howling maelstrom that was Jupiter and had not returned. They had walked into the keening gale — or rather, they had loped, bellies low against the ground, wet sides gleaming in the rain.

For they did not go in the shape of men.

Now the fifth man stood before the desk of Kent Fowler, head of Dome No. 3, Jovian Survey Commission.

Under Fowler's desk, old Towser scratched a flea, then settled down to sleep again.

Harold Allen, Fowler saw with a sudden pang, was young — too young. He had the easy confidence of youth, the straight back and eyes, the face of one who never had known fear. And that was strange. For men in the domes of Jupiter did know fear — fear and humility. It was hard for Man to reconcile his puny self with the mighty forces of the monstrous planet.

"You understand," said Fowler, "that you need not do this. You understand that you need not go."

It was formula, of course. The other four had been told the same thing, but they had gone. This fifth one, Fowler knew, would go too. But suddenly he felt a dull hope stir within him that Allen wouldn't go.

"When do I start?" asked Allen.

There was a time when Fowler might have taken quiet pride in that answer, but not now. He frowned briefly.

"Within the hour," he said.

Allen stood waiting, quietly.

"Four other men have gone out and have not returned," said Fowler. "You know that, of course. We want you to return. We don't want you going off on any heroic rescue expedition. The main thing, the only thing, is that you come back, that you prove Man can live in a Jovian form. Go to the first survey stake, no farther, then come back. Don't take any chances. Don't investigate anything. Just come back."

Allen nodded. "I understand all that."

"Miss Stanley will operate the converter," Fowler went on. "You need have no fear on that particular point. The other men were converted without mishap. They left the converter in apparently perfect condition. You will be in thoroughly competent hands. Miss Stanley is the best qualified conversion operator in the Solar System. She had had experience on most of the other planets. That is why she's here."

Allen grinned at the woman and Fowler saw something flicker across Miss Stanley's face — something that might have been pity, or rage — or just plain fear. But it was gone again and she was smiling back at the youth who stood before the desk. Smiling in that prim, schoolteacherish way she had of smiling, almost as if she hated herself for doing it.

"I shall be looking forward," said Allen, "to my conversion."

And the way he said it, he made it all a joke, a vast, ironic joke.

But it was no joke.

It was serious business, deadly serious. Upon these tests, Fowler knew, depended the fate of men on Jupiter. If the tests succeeded, the resources of the giant planet would be thrown open. Man would take over Jupiter as he already had taken over the smaller planets. And if they failed —

If they failed, Man would continue to be chained and

hampered by the terrific pressure, the greater force of gravity, the weird chemistry of the planet. He would continue to be shut within the domes, unable to set actual foot upon the planet, unable to see it with direct, unaided vision, forced to rely upon the awkward tractors and the televisor, forced to work with clumsy tools and mechanisms or through the medium of robots that themselves were clumsy.

For Man, unprotected and in his natural form, would be blotted out by Jupiter's terrific pressure of fifteen thousand pounds per square inch, pressure that made Terrestrial sea bottoms seem a vacuum by comparison.

Even the strongest metal Earthmen could devise couldn't exist under pressure such as that, under the pressure and the alkaline rains that forever swept the planet. It grew brittle and flaky, crumbling like clay, or it ran away in little streams and puddles of ammonia salts. Only by stepping up the toughness and strength of that metal, by increasing its electronic tension, could it be made to withstand the weight of thousands of miles of swirling, choking gases that made up the atmosphere. And even when that was done, everything had to be coated with tough quartz to keep away the rain — the bitter rain that was liquid ammonia.

Fowler sat listening to the engines in the sub-floor of the dome. Engines that ran on endlessly, the dome never quiet of them. They had to run and keep on running. For if they stopped, the power flowing into the metal walls of the dome would stop, the electronic tension would ease up and that would be the end of everything.

Towser roused himself under Fowler's desk and scratched another flea, his leg thumping hard against the floor.

"Is there anything else?" asked Allen.

Fowler shook his head. "Perhaps there's something you want to do," he said. "Perhaps you —"

He had meant to say write a letter and he was glad he caught himself quick enough so he didn't say it.

Allen looked at his watch. "I'll be there on time," he said. He swung around and headed for the door.

Fowler knew Miss Stanley was watching him and he didn't want to turn and meet her eyes. He fumbled with a sheaf of papers on the desk before him.

"How long are you going to keep this up?" asked Miss Stanley and she bit off each word with a vicious snap.

He swung around in his chair and faced her then. Her lips were drawn into a straight, thin line, her hair seemed skinned back from her forehead tighter than ever, giving her face that queer, almost startling death-mask quality.

He tried to make his voice cool and level. "As long as there's any need of it," he said. "As long as there's any hope."

"You're going to keep on sentencing them to death," she said. "You're going to keep marching them out face to face with Jupiter. You're going to sit in here safe and comfortable and send them out to die."

"There is no room for sentimentality, Miss Stanley," Fowler said, trying to keep the note of anger from his voice. "You know as well as I do why we're doing this. You realize that Man in his own form simply cannot cope with Jupiter. The only answer is to turn men into the sort of things that can cope with it. We've done it on the other planets.

"If a few men die, but we finally succeed, the price is small. Through the ages men have thrown away their lives on foolish things, for foolish reasons. Why should we hesitate, then, at a little death in a thing as great as this?"

Miss Stanley sat stiff and straight, hands folded in her lap, the lights shining on her graying hair and Fowler, watching her, tried to imagine what she might feel, what she might be thinking. He wasn't exactly afraid of her, but he didn't feel quite comfortable when she was around. Those sharp blue eyes saw too much, her hands looked far too competent. She should be somebody's Aunt sitting in a rocking chair with her knitting needles. But she wasn't. She was the top-notch conversion unit operator in the Solar System and she didn't like the way he was doing things.

"There is something wrong, Mr. Fowler," she declared.

"Precisely," agreed Fowler. "That's why I'm sending young Allen out alone. He may find out what it is."

"And if he doesn't?"

"I'll send someone else."

She rose slowly from her chair, started toward the door, then stopped before his desk.

"Some day," she said, "you will be a great man. You never let a chance go by. This is your chance. You knew it was when this dome was picked for the tests. If you put it through, you'll go up a notch or two. No matter how many men may die, you'll go up a notch or two."

"Miss Stanley," he said and his voice was curt, "young Allen is going out soon. Please be sure that your machine —"

"My machine," she told him, icily, "is not to blame. It operates along the co-ordinates the biologists set up."

He sat hunched at his desk, listening to her footsteps go down the corridor.

What she said was true, of course. The biologists had set up the co-ordinates. But the biologists could be wrong. Just a hairbreadth of difference, one iota of digression and the converter would be sending out something that wasn't the thing they meant to send. A mutant that might crack up, go haywire, come unstuck under some condition or stress of circumstance wholly unsuspected.

For Man didn't know much about what was going on outside. Only what his instruments told him was going on. And the samplings of those happenings furnished by those instruments and mechanisms had been no more than samplings, for Jupiter was unbelievably large and the domes were very few.

Even the work of the biologists in getting the data on the Lopers, apparently the highest form of Jovian life, had

involved more than three years of intensive study and after
that two years of checking to make sure. Work that could
have been done on Earth in a week or two. But work that,
in this case, couldn't be done on Earth at all, for one couldn't
take a Jovian life form to Earth. The pressure here on Jupiter
couldn't be duplicated outside of Jupiter and at Earth
pressure and temperature the Lopers would simply have
disappeared in a puff of gas.

Yet it was work that had to be done if Man ever hoped to
go about Jupiter in the life form of the Lopers. For before
the converter could change a man to another life form, every
detailed physical characteristic of that life form must be
known — surely and positively, with no chance of mistake.

Allen did not come back.

The tractors, combing the nearby terrain, found no trace
of him, unless the skulking thing reported by one of the
drivers had been the missing Earthman in Loper form.

The biologists sneered their most accomplished academic
sneers when Fowler suggested the co-ordinates might be
wrong. Carefully they pointed out, the co-ordinates worked.
When a man was put into the converter and the switch was
thrown, the man became a Loper. He left the machine and
moved away, out of sight, into the soupy atmosphere.

Some quirk, Fowler had suggested; some tiny deviation
from the thing a Loper should be, some minor defect. If there
were, the biologists said, it would take years to find it.

And Fowler knew that they were right.

So there were five men now instead of four and Harold
Allen had walked out into Jupiter for nothing at all. It was
as if he'd never gone so far as knowledge was concerned.

Fowler reached across his desk and picked up the personal
file, a thin sheaf of papers neatly clipped together. It was a
thing he dreaded but a thing he had to do. Somehow the
reason for these strange disappearances must be found. And

there was no other way than to send out more men.

He sat for a moment listening to the howling of the wind above the dome, the everlasting thundering gale that swept across the planet in boiling, twisting wrath.

Was there some threat out there, he asked himself? Some danger they did not know about? Something that lay in wait and gobbled up the Lopers, making no distinction between Lopers that were *bona fide* and Lopers that were men? To the gobblers, of course, it would make no difference.

Or had there been a basic fault in selecting the Lopers as the type of life best fitted for existence on the surface of the planet? The evident intelligence of the Lopers, he knew, had been one factor in that determination. For if the thing Man became did not have capacity for intelligence, Man could not for long retain his own intelligence in such a guise.

Had the biologists let that one factor weigh too heavily, using it to offset some other factor that might be unsatisfactory, even disastrous? It didn't seem likely. Stiffnecked as they might be, the biologists knew their business.

Or was the whole thing impossible, doomed from the very start? Conversion to other life forms had worked on other planets, but that did not necessarily mean it would work on Jupiter. Perhaps Man's intelligence could not function correctly through the sensory apparatus provided Jovian life. Perhaps the Lopers were so alien there was no common ground for human knowledge and the Jovian conception of existence to meet and work together.

Or the fault might lie with Man, be inherent with the race. Some mental aberration which, coupled with what they found outside, wouldn't let them come back. Although it might not be an aberration, not in the human sense. Perhaps just one ordinary human mental trait, accepted as commonplace on Earth, would be so violently at odds with Jovian existence that it would blast all human intelligence and sanity.

Claws rattled and clicked down the corridor. Listening to them, Fowler smiled wanly. It was Towser coming back from the kitchen, where he had gone to see his friend, the cook.

Towser came into the room, carrying a bone. He wagged his tail at Fowler and flopped down beside the desk, bone between his paws. For a long moment his rheumy old eyes regarded his master and Fowler reached down a hand to ruffle a ragged ear.

"You still like me, Towser?" Fowler asked and Towser thumped his tail.

"You're the only one," said Fowler. "All through the dome they're cussing me. Calling me a murderer, more than likely."

He straightened and swung back to the desk. His hand reached out and picked up the file.

Bennett? Bennett had a girl waiting for him back on Earth.

Andrews? Andrews was planning on going back to Mars Tech just as soon as he earned enough to see him through a year.

Olson? Olson was nearing pension age. All the time telling the boys how he was going to settle down and grow roses.

Carefully, Fowler laid the file back on the desk.

Sentencing men to death. Miss Stanley had said that, her pale lips scarcely moving in her parchment face. Marching men out to die while he, Fowler, sat here safe and comfortable.

They were saying it all through the dome, no doubt, especially since Allen had failed to return. They wouldn't say it to his face, of course. Even the man or men he called before this desk and told they were the next to go, wouldn't say it to him.

They would only say: "When do we start?" For that was formula.

But he would see it in their eyes.

He picked up the file again. Bennett, Andrews, Olson. There were others, but there was no use in going on.

Kent Fowler knew that he couldn't do it, couldn't face them, couldn't send more men out to die.

He leaned forward and flipped up the toggle on the inter-communicator.

"Yes, Mr. Fowler."

"Miss Stanley, please."

He waited for Miss Stanley, listening to Towser chewing half-heartedly on the bone. Towser's teeth were getting bad.

"Miss Stanley," said Miss Stanley's voice.

"Just wanted to tell you, Miss Stanley, to get ready for two more."

"Aren't you afraid," asked Miss Stanley, "that you'll run out of them? Sending out one at a time, they'd last longer, give you twice the satisfaction."

"One of them," said Fowler, "will be a dog."

"A dog!"

"Yes, Towser."

He heard the quick, cold rage that iced her voice. "Your own dog! He's been with you all these years —"

"That's the point," said Fowler. "Towser would be unhappy if I left him behind."

It was not the Jupiter he had known through the televisor. He had expected it to be different, but not like this. He had expected a hell of ammonia rain and stinking fumes and the deafening, thundering tumult of the storm. He had expected swirling clouds and fog and the snarling flicker of monstrous thunderbolts.

He had not expected the lashing downpour would be reduced to drifting purple mist that moved like fleeing shadows over a red and purple sward. He had not even guessed the snaking bolts of lightning would be flares of pure ecstasy across a painted sky.

Waiting for Towser, Fowler flexed the muscles of his body, amazed at the smooth, sleek strength he found. Not a bad body, he decided, and grimaced at remembering how he had pitied the Lopers when he glimpsed them through the television screen.

For it had been hard to imagine a living organism based upon ammonia and hydrogen rather than upon water and oxygen, hard to believe that such a form of life could know the same quick thrill of life that humankind could know. Hard to conceive of life out in the soupy maelstrom that was Jupiter, not knowing, of course, that through Jovian eyes it was no soupy maelstrom at all.

The wind brushed against him with what seemed gentle fingers and he remembered with a start that by Earth standards the wind was a roaring gale, a two-hundred-mile an hour howler laden with deadly gases.

Pleasant scents seeped into his body. And yet scarcely scents, for it was not the sense of smell as he remembered it. It was as if his whole being was soaking up the sensation of lavender — and yet not lavender. It was something, he knew, for which he had no word, undoubtedly the first of many enigmas in terminology. For the words he knew, the thought symbols that served him as an Earthman would not serve him as a Jovian.

The lock in the side of the dome opened and Towser came tumbling out — at least he thought it must be Towser.

He started to call to the dog, his mind shaping the words he meant to say. But he couldn't say them. There was no way to say them. He had nothing to say them with.

For a moment his mind swirled in muddy terror, a blind fear that eddied in little puffs of panic through his brain.

How did Jovians talk? How —

Suddenly he was aware of Towser, intensely aware of the bumbling, eager friendliness of the shaggy animal that had followed him from Earth to many planets. As if the thing that was Towser had reached out and for a moment sat within his brain.

And out of the bubbling welcome that he sensed, came words.

"Hiya, pal."

Not words really, better than words. Thought symbols in his brain, communicated thought symbols that had shades of meaning words could never have.

"Hiya, Towser," he said.

"I feel good," said Towser. "Like I was a pup. Lately I've been feeling pretty punk. Legs stiffening up on me and teeth wearing down to almost nothing. Hard to mumble a bone with teeth like that. Besides, the fleas give me hell. Used to be I never paid much attention to them. A couple of fleas more or less never meant much in my early days."

"But . . . but —" Fowler's thoughts tumbled awkwardly. "You're talking to me!"

"Sure thing," said Towser. "I always talked to you, but you couldn't hear me. I tried to say things to you, but I couldn't make the grade."

"I understood you sometimes," Fowler said.

"Not very well," said Towser. "You knew when I wanted food and when I wanted a drink and when I wanted out, but that's about all you ever managed."

"I'm sorry," Fowler said.

"Forget it," Towser told him. "I'll race you to the cliff."

For the first time, Fowler saw the cliff, apparently many miles away, but with a strange crystalline beauty that sparkled in the shadow of the many-colored clouds.

Fowler hesitated. "It's a long way —"

"Ah, come on," said Towser and even as he said it he started for the cliff.

Fowler followed, testing his legs, testing the strength in that new body of his, a bit doubtful at first, amazed a moment later, then running with a sheer joyousness that was one with the red and purple sward, with the drifting smoke of the rain across the land.

As he ran the consciousness of music came to him, a music that beat into his body, that surged throughout his being, that lifted him on wings of silver speed. Music like bells might make from some steeple on a sunny, springtime hill.

As the cliff drew nearer the music deepened and filled the universe with a spray of magic sound. And he knew the music came from the tumbling waterfall that feathered down the face of the shining cliff.

Only, he knew, it was no waterfall, but an ammonia-fall and the cliff was white because it was oxygen, solidified.

He skidded to a stop beside Towser where the waterfall broke into a glittering rainbow of many hundred colors. Literally many hundred, for here, he saw, was no shading of one primary to another as human beings saw, but a clear-cut selectivity that broke the prism down to its last ultimate classification.

"The music," said Towser.

"Yes, what about it?"

"The music," said Towser, "is vibrations. Vibrations of water falling."

"But, Towser, you don't know about vibrations."

"Yes, I do," contended Towser. "It just popped into my head."

Fowler gulped mentally. "Just popped!"

And suddenly, within his own head, he held a formula — the formula for a process that would make metal to withstand the pressure of Jupiter.

He stared, astounded, at the waterfall and swiftly his mind took the many colors and placed them in their exact sequence in the spectrum. Just like that. Just out of blue sky. Out of nothing, for he knew nothing either of metals or of colors.

"Towser," he cried. "Towser, something's happening to us!"

"Yeah, I know," said Towser.

"It's our brains," said Fowler. "We're using them, all of

them, down to the last hidden corner. Using them to figure out things we should have known all the time. Maybe the brains of Earth things naturally are slow and foggy. Maybe we are the morons of the universe. Maybe we are fixed so we have to do things the hard way."

And, in the new sharp clarity of thought that seemed to grip him, he knew that it would not only be the matter of colors in a waterfall or metals that would resist the pressure of Jupiter, he sensed other things, things not yet quite clear. A vague whispering that hinted of greater things, of mysteries beyond the pale of human thought, beyond even the pale of human imagination. Mysteries, fact, logic built on reasoning. Things that any brain should know if it used all its reasoning power.

"We're still mostly Earth," he said. "We're just beginning to learn a few of the things we are to know — a few of the things that were kept from us as human beings, perhaps because we were human beings. Because our human bodies were poor bodies. Poorly equipped for thinking, poorly equipped in certain senses that one has to have to know. Perhaps even lacking in certain senses that are necessary to true knowledge."

He stared back at the dome, a tiny black thing dwarfed by the distance.

Back there were men who couldn't see the beauty that was Jupiter. Men who thought that swirling clouds and lashing rain obscured the face of the planet. Unseeing human eyes. Poor eyes. Eyes that could not see the beauty in the clouds, that could not see through the storms. Bodies that could not feel the thrill of trilling music stemming from the rush of broken water.

Men who walked alone, in terrible loneliness, talking with their tongue like Boy Scouts wigwagging out their messages, unable to reach out and touch one another's mind as he could reach out and touch Towser's mind. Shut off forever from that personal, intimate contact with other living things.

He, Fowler, had expected terror inspired by alien things out here on the surface, had expected to cower before the threat of unknown things, had steeled himself against disgust of a situation that was not of Earth.

But instead he had found something greater than Man had ever known. A swifter, surer body. A sense of exhilaration, a deeper sense of life. A sharper mind. A world of beauty that even the dreamers of the Earth had not yet imagined.

"Let's get going," Towser urged.

"Where do you want to go?"

"Anywhere," said Towser. "Just start going and see where we end up. I have a feeling . . . well, a feeling —"

"Yes, I know," said Fowler.

For he had the feeling, too. The feeling of high destiny. A certain sense of greatness. A knowledge that somewhere off beyond the horizons lay adventure and things greater than adventure.

Those other five had felt it, too. Had felt the urge to go and see, the compelling sense that here lay a life of fullness and of knowledge.

That, he knew, was why they had not returned.

"I won't go back," said Towser.

"We can't let them down," said Fowler.

Fowler took a step or two, back toward the dome, then stopped.

Back to the dome. Back to that aching, poison-laden body he had left. It hadn't seemed aching before, but now he knew it was.

Back to the fuzzy brain. Back to muddled thinking. Back to the flapping mouths that formed signals others understood. Back to eyes that now would be worse than no sight at all. Back to squalor, back to crawling, back to ignorance.

"Perhaps some day," he said, muttering to himself.

"We got a lot to do and a lot to see," said Towser. "We got a lot to learn. We'll find things —"

Yes, they could find things. Civilizations, perhaps. Civilizations that would make the civilization of Man seem puny by comparison. Beauty and more important — an understanding of that beauty. And a comradeship no one had ever known before — that no man, no dog had ever known before.

And life. The quickness of life after what seemed a drugged existence.

"I can't go back," said Towser.

"Nor I," said Fowler.

"They would turn me back into a dog," said Towser.

"And me," said Fowler, "back into a man."

In "A Bad Day for Sales," Fritz Leiber uses dark comedy to create an unforgettable end-of-the world story.

A BAD DAY FOR SALES

FRITZ LEIBER

The big bright doors of the office building parted with a pneumatic *whoosh* and Robie glided onto Times Square. The crowd that had been watching the fifty-foot-tall girl on the clothing billboard get dressed, or reading the latest news about the Hot Truce scrawl itself in yard-high script, hurried to look.

Robie was still a novelty. Robie was fun. For a little while yet, he could steal the show. But the attention did not make Robie proud. He had no more emotions than the pink plastic giantess, who dressed and undressed endlessly whether there was a crowd or the street was empty, and who never once blinked her blue mechanical eyes. But she merely drew business while Robie went out after it.

For Robie was the logical conclusion of the development of vending machines. All the earlier ones had stood in one place, on a floor or hanging on a wall, and blankly delivered merchandise in return for coins, whereas Robie searched for customers. He was the demonstration model of a line of sales robots to be manufactured by Shuler Vending Machines, provided the public invested enough in stocks to give the company capital to go into mass production.

The publicity Robie drew stimulated investments hand-somely. It was amusing to see the TV and newspaper coverage of Robie selling, but not a fraction as much fun as being approached personally by him. Those who were usually bought anywhere from one to five hundred shares, if they had any money and foresight enough to see that sales robots would eventually be on every street and highway in the country.

Robie radared the crowd, found that it surrounded him solidly and stopped. With a carefully built-in sense of timing, he waited for the tension and expectation to mount before he began talking.

"Say, Ma, he doesn't look like a robot at all," a child said. "He looks like a turtle."

Which was not completely inaccurate. The lower part of Robie's body was a metal hemisphere hemmed with sponge rubber and not quite touching the sidewalk. The upper was a metal box with black holes in it. The box could swivel and duck.

A chromium-bright hoopskirt with a turret on top.

"Reminds me too much of the Little Joe Paratanks," a legless veteran of the Persian War muttered, and rapidly rolled himself away on wheels rather like Robie's.

His departure made it easier for some of those who knew about Robie to open a path in the crowd. Robie headed straight for the gap. The crowd whooped.

Robie glided very slowly down the path, deftly jogging aside whenever he got too close to ankles in skylon or sockassins. The rubber buffer on his hoopskirt was merely an added safeguard.

The boy who had called Robie a turtle jumped in the middle of the path and stood his ground, grinning foxily.

Robie stopped two feet short of him. The turret ducked. The crowd got quiet.

"Hello, youngster," Robie said in a voice that was smooth as that of a TV star, and was, in fact, a recording of one.

The boy stopped smiling. "Hello," he whispered.

"How old are you?" Robie asked.

"Nine. No, eight."

"That's nice," Robie observed. A metal arm shot down from his neck, stopped just short of the boy.

The boy jerked back.

"For you," Robie said.

The boy gingerly took the red polly-lop from the neatly fashioned blunt metal claws, and began to unwrap it.

"Nothing to say?" asked Robie.

"Uh — thank you."

After a suitable pause, Robie continued, "And how about a nice refreshing drink of Poppy Pop to go with your polly-lop?" The boy lifted his eyes, but didn't stop licking the candy. Robie waggled his claws slightly. "Just give me a quarter and within five seconds —"

A little girl wriggled out of the forest of legs. "Give me a polly-lop, too, Robie," she demanded.

"Rita, come back here!" a woman in the third rank of the crowd called angrily.

Robie scanned the newcomer gravely. His reference silhouettes were not good enough to let him distinguish the sex of children, so he merely repeated, "Hello, youngster."

"Rita!"

"Give me a polly-lop!"

Disregarding both remarks, for a good salesman is singleminded and does not waste bait, Robie said winningly, "I'll bet you read *Junior Space Killers*. Now I have here —"

"Uh-uh, I'm a girl. *He* got a polly-lop."

At the word "girl," Robie broke off. Rather ponderously, he said, "I'll bet you read *Gee-Gee Jones, Space Stripper*. Now I have here the latest issue of that thrilling comic, not yet in the stationary vending machines. Just give me fifty cents and within five —"

"Please let me through. I'm her mother."

A young woman in the front rank drawled over her powder-sprayed shoulder, "I'll get her for you," and slithered out on six-inch platform shoes. "Run away, children," she said nonchalantly. Lifting her arms behind her head, she pirouetted slowly before Robie to show how much she did for her bolero half-jacket and her form-fitting slacks that melted into skylon just above the knees. The little girl glared at her. She ended the pirouette in profile.

At this age-level, Robie's reference silhouettes permitted him to distinguish sex, though with occasional amusing and embarrassing miscalls. He whistled admiringly. The crowd cheered.

Someone remarked critically to a friend, "It would go over better if he was built more like a real robot. You know, like a man."

The friend shook his head. "This way it's subtler."

No one in the crowd was watching the newscript overhead as it scribbled, "Ice Pack for Hot Truce? Vanahdin hints Russ may yield on Pakistan."

Robie was saying, " . . . in the savage new glamor-tint we have christened Mars Blood, complete with spray applicator and fit-all fingerstalls that mask each finger completely except for the nail. Just give me five dollars — uncrumpled bills may be fed into the revolving rollers you see beside my arm — and within five seconds —"

"No, thanks, Robie," the young woman yawned.

"Remember," Robie persisted, "for three more weeks, seductivizing Mars Blood will be unobtainable from any other robot or human vendor."

"No, thanks."

Robie scanned the crowd resourcefully. "Is there any gentleman here . . . " he began just as a woman elbowed her way through the front rank.

"I told you to come back!" she snapped at the little girl.

"But I didn't get my polly-lop!"

" . . . who would care to . . . "

"Rita!"

"Robie cheated. Ow!"

Meanwhile, the young woman in the half-bolero had scanned the nearby gentlemen on her own. Deciding that there was less than a fifty per cent chance of any of them accepting the proposition Robie seemed about to make, she took advantage of the scuffle to slither gracefully back into the ranks. Once again the path was clear before Robie.

He paused, however, for a brief recapitulation of the more magical properties of Mars Blood, including a telling phrase about "the passionate claws of a Martian sunrise."

But no one bought. It wasn't quite time. Soon enough silver coins would be clinking, bills going through the rollers faster than laundry, and five hundred people struggling for the privilege of having their money taken away from them by America's first mobile sales robot.

But there were still some tricks that Robie had to do free, and one certainly should enjoy those before starting the more expensive fun.

So Robie moved on until he reached the curb. The variation in level was instantly sensed by his underscanners. He stopped. His head began to swivel. The crowd watched in eager silence. This was Robie's best trick.

Robie's head stopped swiveling. His scanners had found the traffic light. It was green. Robie edged forward. But then the light turned red. Robie stopped again, still on the curb. The crowd softly *ahhed* its delight.

It was wonderful to be alive and watching Robie on such an exciting day. Alive and amused in the fresh, weather-controlled air between the lines of bright skyscrapers with their winking windows and under a sky so blue you could almost call it dark.

(But way, way up, where the crowd could not see, the sky was darker still. Purple-dark, with stars showing. And in that purple-dark, a silver-green something, the color of a bud, plunged down at better than three miles a second. The silver-green was a newly developed paint that foiled radar.)

Robie was saying, "While we wait for the light, there's time for you youngsters to enjoy a nice refreshing Poppy

Pop. Or for you adults — only those over five feet tall are eligible to buy — to enjoy an exciting Poppy Pop fizz. Just give me a quarter or — in the case of adults, one dollar and a quarter; I'm licensed to dispense intoxicating liquors — and within five seconds . . . "

But that was not cutting it quite fine enough. Just three seconds later, the silver-green bud bloomed above Manhattan into a globular orange flower. The skyscrapers grew brighter and brighter still, the brightness of the inside of the Sun. The windows winked blossoming white fire-flowers.

The crowd around Robie bloomed, too. Their clothes puffed into petals of flame. Their heads of hair were torches.

The orange flower grew, stem and blossom. The blast came. The winking windows shattered tier by tier, became black holes. The walls bent, rocked, cracked. A stony dandruff flaked from their cornices. The flaming flowers on the sidewalk were all leveled at once. Robie was shoved ten feet. His metal hoopskirt dimpled, regained its shape.

The blast ended. The orange flower, grown vast, vanished overhead on its huge, magic beanstalk. It grew dark and very still. The cornice-dandruff pattered down. A few small fragments rebounded from the metal hoopskirt.

Robie made some small, uncertain movements, as if feeling for broken bones. He was hunting for the traffic light, but it no longer shone either red or green.

He slowly scanned a full circle. There was nothing anywhere to interest his reference silhouettes. Yet whenever he tried to move, his under-scanners warned him of low obstructions. It was very puzzling.

The silence was disturbed by moans and a crackling sound, as faint at first as the scampering of distant rats.

A seared man, his charred clothes fuming where the blast had blown out the fire, rose from the curb. Robie scanned him.

"Good day, sir," Robie said. "Would you care for a

smoke? A truly cool smoke? Now I have here a yet-unmar-
keted brand . . . "

But the customer had run away, screaming, and Robie
never ran after customers, though he could follow them at a
medium brisk roll. He worked his way along the curb where
the man had sprawled, carefully keeping his distance from
the low obstructions, some of which writhed now and then,
forcing him to jog. Shortly he reached a fire hydrant. He
scanned it. His electronic vision, though it still worked, had
been somewhat blurred by the blast.

"Hello, youngster," Robie said. Then, after a long pause,
"Cat got your tongue? Well, I have a little present for you.
A nice, lovely polly-lop.

"Take it, youngster," he said after another pause. "It's for
you. Don't be afraid."

His attention was distracted by other customers, who
began to rise oddly here and there, twisting forms that
confused his reference silhouettes and would not stay to be
scanned properly. One cried, "Water," but no quarter
clinked in Robie's claws when he caught the word and suggested, "How about a nice refreshing drink of Poppy Pop?"

The rat-crackling of the flames had become a jungle
muttering. The blind windows began to wink fire again.

A little girl marched, stepping neatly over arms and legs
she did not look at. A white dress and the once taller bodies
around her had shielded her from the brilliance and the blast.
Her eyes were fixed on Robie. In them was the same
imperious confidence, though none of the delight, with which
she had watched him earlier.

"Help me, Robie," she said. "I want my mother."

"Hello, youngster," Robie said. "What would you like?
Comics? Candy?"

"Where is she, Robie? Take me to her."

"Balloons? Would you like to watch me blow up a bal-
loon?"

The little girl began to cry. The sound triggered off another of Robie's novelty circuits, a service feature that had brought in a lot of favorable publicity.

"Is something wrong?" he asked. "Are you in trouble? Are you lost?"

"Yes, Robie. Take me to my mother."

"Stay right here," Robie said reassuringly, "and don't be frightened. I will call a policeman." He whistled shrilly, twice.

Time passed. Robie whistled again. The windows flared and roared. The little girl begged, "Take me away, Robie," and jumped onto a little step in his hoopskirt.

"Give me a dime," Robie said.

The little girl found one in her pocket and put it in his claws.

"Your weight," Robie said, "is fifty-four and one-half pounds."

"Have you seen my daughter, have you seen her?" a woman was crying somewhere. "I left her watching that thing while I stepped inside — Rita!"

"Robie helped me," the little girl began babbling at her. "He knew I was lost. He even called the police, but they didn't come. He weighed me, too. Didn't you, Robie?"

But Robie had gone off to peddle Poppy Pop to the members of a rescue squad which had just come around the corner, more robotlike in their asbestos suits than he in his metal skin.

Who is Mr. Underhill, and what is his secret? In this story,
Ursula K. Le Guin brings to life a fantasy world of wizards,
dragons, and mystery.

THE RULE OF NAMES

URSULA K. LE GUIN

Mr. Underhill came out from under his hill, smiling and
breathing hard. Each breath shot out of his nostrils as a
double puff of steam, snow-white in the morning sunshine.
Mr. Underhill looked up at the bright December sky and
smiled wider than ever, showing snow-white teeth. Then he
went down to the village.

"Morning, Mr. Underhill," said the villagers as he passed
them in the narrow street between houses with conical,
overhanging roofs like the fat red caps of toadstools.
"Morning, morning!" he replied to each. (It was of course
bad luck to wish anyone a *good* morning; a simple statement
of the time of day was quite enough, in a place so permeated
with Influences as Sattins Island, where a careless adjective
might change the weather for a week.) All of them spoke to
him, some with affection, some with affectionate disdain. He
was all the little island had in the way of a wizard, and so
deserved respect — but how could you respect a little fat
man of fifty who waddled along with his toes turned in,
breathing steam and smiling? He was no great shakes as a
workman either. His fireworks were fairly elaborate but his
elixirs were weak. Warts he charmed off frequently reap-
peared after three days; tomatoes he enchanted grew no
bigger than canteloupes; and those rare times when a strange
ship stopped at Sattins Harbor, Mr. Underhill always stayed
under his hill — for fear, he explained, of the evil eye. He

was, in other words, a wizard the way walleyed Gan was a carpenter: by default. The villagers made do with badly-hung doors and inefficient spells, for this generation, and relieved their annoyance by treating Mr. Underhill quite familiarly, as a mere fellow-villager. They even asked him to dinner. Once he asked some of them to dinner, and served a splendid repast, with silver, crystal, damask, roast goose, sparkling Andrades '639, and plum pudding with hard sauce; but he was so nervous all through the meal that it took the joy out of it, and besides, everybody was hungry again half an hour afterward. He did not like anyone to visit his cave, not even the anteroom, beyond which in fact nobody had ever got. When he saw people approaching the hill he always came trotting out to meet them. "Let's sit out here under the pine trees!" he would say, smiling and waving towards the fir grove, or if it was raining, "Let's go have a drink at the inn, eh?" though everybody knew he drank nothing stronger than well-water.

Some of the village children, teased by that locked cave, poked and pried and made raids while Mr. Underhill was away; but the small door that led into the inner chamber was spell-shut, and it seemed for once to be an effective spell. Once a couple of boys, thinking the wizard was over on the West Shore curing Mrs. Ruuna's sick donkey, brought a crowbar and a hatchet up there, but at the first whack of the hatchet on the door there came a roar of wrath from inside, and a cloud of purple steam. Mr. Underhill had got home early. The boys fled. He did not come out, and the boys came to no harm, though they said you couldn't believe what a huge hooting howling hissing horrible bellow that little fat man could make unless you'd heard it.

His business in town this day was three dozen fresh eggs and a pound of liver; also a stop at Seacaptain Fogeno's cottage to renew the seeing-charm on the old man's eyes (quite useless when applied to a case of detached retina, but

Mr. Underhill kept trying), and finally a chat with old Goody
Guld, the concertina-maker's widow. Mr. Underhill's friends
were mostly old people. He was timid with the strong young
men of the village, and the girls were shy of him. "He makes
me nervous, he smiles so much," they all said, pouting,
twisting silky ringlets round a finger. "Nervous" was a
newfangled word, and their mothers all replied grimly,
"Nervous my foot, silliness is the word for it. Mr. Underhill
is a very respectable wizard!"

After leaving Goody Guld, Mr. Underhill passed by the
school, which was being held this day out on the common.
Since no one on Sattins Island was literate, there were no
books to learn to read from and no desks to carve initials on
and no blackboards to erase, and in fact no schoolhouse. On
rainy days the children met in the loft of the Communal
Barn, and got hay in their pants; on sunny days the school-
teacher, Palani, took them anywhere she felt like. Today,
surrounded by thirty interested children under twelve and
forty uninterested sheep under five, she was teaching an
important item on the curriculum: the Rules of Names. Mr.
Underhill, smiling shyly, paused to listen and watch. Palani,
a plump, pretty girl of twenty, made a charming picture there
in the wintry sunlight, sheep and children around her, a
leafless oak above her, and behind her the dunes and sea and
clear, pale sky. She spoke earnestly, her face flushed pink by
wind and words. "Now you know the Rules of Names
already, children. There are two, and they're the same on
every island in the world. What's one of them?"

"It ain't polite to ask anybody what his name is," shouted
a fat, quick boy, interrupted by a little girl shrieking, "You
can't never tell your own name to nobody my ma says!"

"Yes, Suba. Yes, Popi dear, don't screech. That's right.
You never ask anybody his name. You never tell your own.
Now think about that a minute and then tell me why we call
our wizard Mr. Underhill." She smiled across the curly heads

and the woolly backs at Mr. Underhill, who beamed, and nervously clutched his sack of eggs.

"'Cause he lives under a hill!" said half the children.

"But is it his truename?"

"No!" said the fat boy, echoed by little Popi shrieking, "No!"

"How do you know it's not?"

"'Cause he came here all alone and so there wasn't anybody knew his truename so they couldn't tell us, and *he* couldn't —"

"Very good, Suba. Popi, don't shout. That's right. Even a wizard can't tell his truename. When you children are through school and go through the Passage, you'll leave your childnames behind and keep only your truenames, which you must never ask for and never give away. Why is that the rule?"

The children were silent. The sheep bleated gently. Mr. Underhill answered the question: "Because the name is the thing," he said in his shy, soft, husky voice, "and the truename is the true thing. To speak the name is to control the thing. Am I right, Schoolmistress?"

She smiled and curtseyed, evidently a little embarrassed by his participation. And he trotted off towards his hill, clutching his eggs to his bosom. Somehow the minute spent watching Palani and the children had made him very hungry. He locked his inner door behind him with a hasty incantation, but there must have been a leak or two in the spell, for soon the bare anteroom of the cave was rich with the smell of frying eggs and sizzling liver.

The wind that day was light and fresh out of the west, and on it at noon a little boat came skimming the bright waves into Sattins Harbor. Even as it rounded the point a sharp-eyed boy spotted it, and knowing, like every child on the island, every sail and spar of the forty boats of the fishing fleet, he ran down the street calling out, "A foreign boat, a foreign boat!" Very seldom was the lonely isle visited by a boat from some equally lonely isle of the East Reach, or an adventurous trader from the Archipelago. By the time the boat was at the pier half the village was there to greet it, and fishermen were following it homewards, and cowherds and clam-diggers and herb-hunters were puffing up and down all the rocky hills, heading towards the harbor.

But Mr. Underhill's door stayed shut.

There was only one man aboard the boat. Old Seacaptain Fogeno, when they told him that, drew down a bristle of white brows over his unseeing eyes. "There's only one kind of man," he said, "that sails the Outer Reach alone. A wizard, or a warlock, or a Mage . . . "

So the villagers were breathless hoping to see for once in their lives a Mage, one of the mighty White Magicians of the rich, towered, crowded inner islands of the Archipelago. They were disappointed, for the voyager was quite young, a handsome black-bearded fellow who hailed them cheerfully from his boat, and leaped ashore like any sailor glad to have made port. He introduced himself at once as a sea-peddlar. But when they told Seacaptain Fogeno that he carried an oaken walking-stick around with him, the old man nodded. "Two wizards in one town," he said. "Bad!" And his mouth snapped shut like an old carp's.

As the stranger could not give them his name, they gave him one right away: Blackbeard. And they gave him plenty of attention. He had a small mixed cargo of cloth and sandals and piswi feathers for trimming cloaks and cheap incense and levity stones and fine herbs and great glass beads from Venway — the usual peddlar's lot. Everyone on Sattins Island came to look, to chat with the voyager, and perhaps to buy something — "Just to remember him by!" cackled Goody Guld, who like all the women and girls of the village was smitten with Blackbeard's bold good looks. All the boys hung round him too, to hear him tell of his voyages to far, strange islands of the Reach or describe the great rich islands of the Archipelago, the Inner Lanes, the roadsteads white with ships, and the golden roofs of Havnor. The men willingly listened to his tales; but some of them wondered why a trader should sail alone, and kept their eyes thoughtfully upon his oaken staff.

But all this time Mr. Underhill stayed under his hill.

"This is the first island I've ever seen that had no wizard," said Blackbeard one evening to Goody Guld, who had invited him and her nephew and Palani in for a cup of rushwash tea. "What do you do when you get a toothache, or the cow goes dry?"

"Why, we've got Mr. Underhill!" said the old woman.

"For what that's worth," muttered her nephew Birt, and then blushed purple and spilled his tea. Birt was a fisherman, a large, brave, wordless young man. He loved the schoolmistress, but the nearest he had come to telling her of his love was to give baskets of fresh mackerel to her father's cook.

"Oh, you do have a wizard?" Blackbeard asked. "Is he invisible?"

"No, he's just very shy," said Palani. "You've only been here a week, you know, and we see so few strangers here. . . ." She also blushed a little, but did not spill her tea.

Blackbeard smiled at her. "He's a good Sattinsman, then, eh?"

"No," said Goody Guld, "no more than you are. Another cup, nevvy? Keep it in the cup this time. No, my dear, he came in a little bit of a boat, four years ago was it? Just a day after the end of the shad run, I recall, for they was taking up the nets over in East Creek, and Pondi Cowherd broke his leg that very morning — five years ago it must be. No, four. No, five it is, 'twas the year the garlic didn't sprout. So he sails in on a bit of a sloop loaded full up with great chests and boxes and says to Seacaptain Fogeno, who wasn't blind then, though old enough goodness knows to be blind twice over, 'I hear tell,' he says, ' you've got no wizard nor warlock at all, might you be wanting one?' 'Indeed, if the magic's white!' says the Captain, and before you could say cuttlefish Mr. Underhill had settled down in the cave under the hill and was charming the mange off Goody Beltow's cat. Though the fur grew in grey, and 'twas an orange cat. Queer-looking thing it was after that. It died last winter in the cold spell. Goody Beltow took on so at that cat's death, poor thing, worse than when her man was drowned on the Long Banks, the year of the long herring-runs, when nevvy Birt here was but a babe in petticoats." Here Birt spilled his tea again, and Blackbeard grinned, but Goody Guld proceeded undismayed, and talked on till nightfall.

Next day Blackbeard was down at the pier, seeing after the sprung board in his boat which he seemed to take a long time fixing, and as usual drawing the taciturn Sattinsmen into talk. "Now which of these is your wizard's craft?" he asked. "Or has he got one of those the Mages fold up into a walnut shell when they're not using it?"

"Nay," said a stolid fisherman. "She's oop in his cave, under hill."

"He carried the boat he came in up to his cave?"

"Aye. Clear oop. I helped. Heavier as lead she was. Full oop with great boxes, and they full oop with books o' spells, he says. Heavier as lead she was." And the stolid fisherman turned his back, sighing stolidly. Goody Guld's nephew, mending a net nearby, looked up from his work and asked with equal stolidity, "Would ye like to meet Mr. Underhill, maybe?"

Blackbeard returned Birt's look. Clever black eyes met candid blue ones for a long moment; then Blackbeard smiled and said, "Yes. Will you take me up to the hill, Birt?"

"Aye, when I'm done with this," said the fisherman. And when the net was mended, he and the Archipelagan set off up the village street towards the high green hill above it. But

as they crossed the common Blackbeard said, "Hold on a
while, friend Birt. I have a tale to tell you, before we meet
your wizard."

"Tell away," says Birt, sitting down in the shade of a live-
oak.

"It's a story that started a hundred years ago, and isn't
finished yet — though it soon will be, very soon. . . . In the
very heart of the Archipelago, where the islands crowd thick
as flies on honey, there's a little isle called Pendor. The
sealords of Pendor were mighty men, in the old days of war
before the League. Loot and ransom and tribute came
pouring into Pendor, and they gathered a great treasure there,
long ago. Then from somewhere away out in the West Reach,
where dragons breed on the lava isles, came one day a very
mighty dragon. Not one of those overgrown lizards most
of you Outer Reach folk call dragons, but a big, black,
winged, wise, cunning monster, full of strength and subtlety,
and like all dragons loving gold and precious stones above
all things. He killed the Sealord and his soldiers, and the
people of Pendor fled in their ships by night. They all fled
away and left the dragon coiled up in Pendor Towers.
And there he stayed for a hundred years, dragging his scaly
belly over the emeralds and sapphires and coins of gold, coming forth only once in a year or two when he must eat.
He'd raid nearby islands for his food. You know what dragons eat?"

Birt nodded and said in a whisper, "Maidens."

"Right," said Blackbeard. "Well, that couldn't be endured
forever, nor the thought of him sitting on all that treasure.
So after the League grew strong, and the Archipelago wasn't
so busy with wars and piracy, it was decided to attack
Pendor, drive out the dragon, and get the gold and jewels for
the treasury of the League. They're forever wanting money,
the League is. So a huge fleet gathered from fifty islands, and
seven Mages stood in the prows of the seven strongest ships,

and they sailed towards Pendor. . . . They got there. They landed. Nothing stirred. The houses all stood empty, the dishes on the tables full of a hundred years' dust. The bones of the old Sealord and his men lay about in the castle courts and on the stairs. And the Tower rooms reeked of dragon. But there was no dragon. And no treasure, not a diamond the size of a poppyseed, not a single silver bead. . . . Knowing that he couldn't stand up to seven Mages, the dragon had skipped out. They tracked him, and found he'd flown to a deserted island up north called Udrath; they followed his trail there, and what did they find? Bones again. His bones — the dragon's. But no treasure. A wizard, some unknown wizard from somewhere, must have met him single-handed, and defeated him — and then made off with the treasure, right under the League's nose!"

The fisherman listened, attentive and expressionless.

"Now that must have been a powerful wizard and a clever one, first to kill a dragon, and second to get off without leaving a trace. The lords and Mages of the Archipelago couldn't track him at all, neither where he'd come from nor where he'd made off to. They were about to give up. That was last spring; I'd been off on a three-year voyage up in the North Reach, and got back about that time. And they asked me to help them find the unknown wizard. That was clever of them. Because I'm not only a wizard myself, as I think some of the oafs here have guessed, but I am also a descendant of the Lords of Pendor. That treasure is mine. It's mine, and knows that it's mine. Those fools of the League couldn't find it, because it's not theirs. It belongs to the House of Pendor, and the great emerald, the star of the hoard, Inalkil the Greenstone, knows its master. Behold!" Blackbeard raised his oaken staff and cried aloud, "Inalkil!" The tip of the staff began to glow green, a fiery green radiance, a dazzling haze the color of April grass, and at the same moment the staff tipped in the wizard's hand, leaning,

slanting till it pointed straight at the side of the hill above
them.

"It wasn't so bright a glow, far away in Havnor,"
Blackbeard murmured, "but the staff pointed true. Inalkil
answered when I called. The jewel knows its master. And I
know the thief, and I shall conquer him. He's a mighty
wizard, who could overcome a dragon. But I am mightier.
Do you want to know why, oaf? Because I know his name!"

As Blackbeard's tone got more arrogant, Birt had looked
duller and duller, blanker and blanker; but at this he gave a
twitch, shut his mouth, and stared at the Archipelagan.
"How did you . . . learn it?" he asked very slowly.

Blackbeard grinned, and did not answer.

"Black magic?"

"How else?"

Birt looked pale, and said nothing.

"I am the Sealord of Pendor, oaf, and I will have the gold
my fathers won, and the jewels my mothers wore, and the
Greenstone! For they are mine. — Now, you can tell your
village boobies the whole story after I have defeated this
wizard and gone. Wait here. Or you can come and watch, if
you're not afraid. You'll never get the chance again to see a
great wizard in all his power." Blackbeard turned, and
without a backward glance strode off up the hill towards the
entrance to the cave.

Very slowly, Birt followed. A good distance from the cave
he stopped, sat down under a hawthorn tree, and watched.
The Archipelagan had stopped; a stiff, dark figure alone on
the green swell of the hill before the gaping cave-mouth, he
stood perfectly still. All at once he swung his staff up over
his head, and the emerald radiance shone about him as he
shouted, "Thief, thief of the Hoard of Pendor, come forth!"

There was a crash, as of dropped crockery, from inside the
cave, and a lot of dust came spewing out. Scared, Birt ducked.
When he looked again he saw Blackbeard still standing

motionless, and at the mouth of the cave, dusty and dishev-
elled, stood Mr. Underhill. He looked small and pitiful, with
his toes turned in as usual, and his little bowlegs in black
tights, and no staff — he never had had one, Birt suddenly
thought. Mr. Underhill spoke. "Who are you?" he said in his
husky little voice.

"I am the Sealord of Pendor, thief, come to claim my
treasure!"

At that, Mr. Underhill slowly turned pink, as he always
did when people were rude to him. But he then turned
something else. He turned yellow. His hair bristled out, he
gave a coughing roar — and was a yellow lion leaping down
the hill at Blackbeard, white fangs gleaming.

But Blackbeard no longer stood there. A gigantic tiger,
color of night and lightning, bounded to meet the lion. . . .

The lion was gone. Below the cave all of a sudden stood a
high grove of trees, black in the winter sunshine. The tiger,
checking himself in mid-leap just before he entered the
shadow of the trees, caught fire in the air, became a tongue
of flame lashing out at the dry black branches. . . .

But where the trees had stood a sudden cataract leaped
from the hillside, an arch of silvery crashing water, thundering down upon the fire. But the fire was gone. . . .

For just a moment before the fisherman's staring eyes two
hills rose — the green one he knew, and a new one, a bare,
brown hillock ready to drink up the rushing waterfall. That
passed so quickly it made Birt blink, and after blinking he
blinked again, and moaned, for what he saw now was a great
deal worse. Where the cataract had been there hovered a
dragon. Black wings darkened all the hill, steel claws reached
groping, and from the dark, scaly, gaping lips fire and steam
shot out.

Beneath the monstrous creature stood Blackbeard, laugh-
ing.

"Take any shape you please, little Mr. Underhill!" he

taunted. "I can match you. But the game grows tiresome. I want to look upon my treasure, upon Inalkil. Now, big dragon, little wizard, take your true shape. I command you by the power of your true name — Yevaud!"

Birt could not move at all, not even to blink. He cowered, staring whether he would or not. He saw the black dragon hang there in the air above Blackbeard. He saw the fire lick like many tongues from the scaly mouth, the steam jet from the red nostrils. He saw Blackbeard's face grow white, white as chalk, and the beard-fringed lips trembling.

"Your name is Yevaud!"

"Yes," said a great, husky, hissing voice. "My truename is Yevaud, and my true shape is this shape."

"But the dragon was killed — they found dragon-bones on Udrath Island —"

"That was another dragon," said the dragon, and then stooped like a hawk, talons outstretched. And Birt shut his eyes.

When he opened them the sky was clear, the hillside empty, except for a reddish-blackish trampled spot, and a few talon-marks in the grass.

Birt the fisherman got to his feet and ran. He ran across the common, scattering sheep to right and left, and straight down the village street to Palani's father's house. Palani was out in the garden weeding the nasturtiums. "Come with me!" Birt gasped. She stared. He grabbed her wrist and dragged her with him. She screeched a little, but did not resist. He ran with her straight to the pier, pushed her into his fishing-sloop the *Queenie*, untied the painter, took up the oars and set off rowing like a demon. The last that Sattins Island saw of him and Palani was the *Queenie*'s sail vanishing in the direction of the nearest island westward.

The villagers thought they would never stop talking about it, how Goody Guld's nephew Birt had lost his mind and sailed off with the schoolmistress on the very same day that the peddlar Blackbeard disappeared without a trace, leaving all his feathers and beads behind. But they did stop talking about it, three days later. They had other things to talk about, when Mr. Underhill finally came out of his cave.

Mr. Underhill had decided that since his truename was no longer a secret, he might as well drop his disguise. Walking was a lot harder than flying, and besides, it was a long, long time since he had had a real meal.

When Martians landed on Earth, Dick was placed in charge of a massive public-relations campaign. His job: to convince humans to accept the snail-like Martians. Did Dick do his job too well?

BETELGEUSE BRIDGE

WILLIAM TENN

You tell them, Alvarez, old boy; you know how to talk to them. This isn't my kind of public relations. All I care about is that they get the pitch exactly right, with all the implications and complications and everything just the way they really were.

If it hurts, well, let them yell. Just use your words and get it right. Get it all.

You can start with the day the alien spaceship landed outside Baltimore. Makes you sick to think how we never tumbled, doesn't it, Alvarez? No more than a hop, skip, and a jet from the Capitol dome, and we thought it was just a lucky accident.

Explain why we thought it was so lucky. Explain about the secrecy it made possible, the farmer who telephoned the news was placed in special and luxurious custody, how a hand-picked cordon of M.P.s paced five square miles off into an emergency military reservation a few hours later, how Congress was called into secret session and the way it was all kept out of the newspapers.

How and why Trowson, my old sociology prof, was consulted once the problem became clear. How he blinked at the brass hats and striped pants and came up with the answer.

Me. I was the answer.

How my entire staff and I were plucked out of our New

York offices, where we were quietly earning a million bucks, by a flying squad of the F.B.I. and air-mailed to Baltimore. Honestly, Alvarez, even after Trowson explained the situation to me, I was still irritated. Government hush-hush always makes me uncomfortable. Though I don't have to tell you how grateful I was for it later.

The spaceship itself was such a big surprise that I didn't even wet my lips when the first of the aliens *slooshed* out. After all those years of streamlined cigar shapes the Sunday supplement artists had dreamed up, that colorful and rococo spheroid rearing out of a barley field in Maryland looked less like an interplanetary vessel than an oversized ornament for a what-not table. Nothing that seemed like a rocket jet anywhere.

"And there's your job." The prof pointed. "Those two visitors."

They were standing on a flat metal plate surrounded by the highest the republic had elected or appointed. Nine feet of slimy green trunk tapering up from a rather wide base to a pointed top, and dressed in a tiny pink-and-white shell. Two stalks with eyes on them that swung this way and that, and seemed muscular enough to throttle a man. And a huge wet slash of a mouth that showed whenever an edge of the squirming base lifted from the metal plate.

"Snails," I said. "*Snails!*"

"Or slugs," Trowson amended. "Gastropodal mollusks in any case." He gestured at the roiling white bush of hair that sprouted from his head. "But, Dick, that vestigial bit of coiled shell is even less an evolutionary memento than this. They're an older — and smarter — race."

"Smarter?"

He nodded. "When our engineers got curious, they were very courteously invited inside to inspect the ship. They came out with their mouths hanging."

I began to get uncomfortable. I ripped a small piece off my

manicure. "Well, naturally, prof, if they're so alien, so different —"

"Not only that. Superior. Get that, Dick, because it'll be very important in what you have to do. The best engineering minds that this country can assemble in a hurry are like a crowd of South Sea Islanders trying to analyze the rifle and compass from what they know of spears and wind storms. These creatures belong to a galaxy-wide civilization composed of races *at least* as advanced as they; we're a bunch of backward hicks in an unfrequented hinterland of space that's about to be opened to exploration. Exploitation, perhaps, if we can't measure up. We have to give a very good impression and we have to learn fast."

A dignified official with a briefcase detached himself from the nodding, smiling group around the aliens and started for us.

"*Whew!*" I commented brilliantly. "Fourteen ninety-two, repeat performance." I thought for a moment, not too clearly. "But why send the Army and Navy after *me*? I'm not going to be able to read blueprints from — from —"

"Betelgeuse. Ninth planet of the star Betelgeuse. No, Dick, we've already had Dr. Warbury out here. They learned English from him in two hours, although he hasn't identified a word of theirs in three days! And people like Lopez, like Mainzer, are going quietly psychotic trying to locate their power source. We have the best minds we can get to do the learning. Your job is different. We want you as a top-notch advertising man, a public-relations executive. You're the good impression part of the program."

The official plucked at my sleeve and I shrugged him away. "Isn't that the function of government glad-handers?" I asked Trowson.

"No. Don't you remember what you said when you first saw them? *Snails!* How do you think this country is going to take to the idea of snails — giant snails — who sneer condescendingly at our skyscraper cities, our atomic bombs, our most advanced mathematics? We're a conceited kind of monkey. Also, we're afraid of the dark."

There was a gentle official tap on my shoulder. I said "*Please!*" impatiently. I watched the warm little breeze ruffle Professor Trowson's slept-in clothes and noticed the tiny red streaks in his weary eyes.

" 'Mighty Monsters from Outer Space.' Headlines like that, Prof?"

"Slugs with superiority complexes. *Dirty* slugs, more likely. We're lucky they landed in this country, and so close to the Capitol too. In a few days we'll have to call in the heads of other nations. Then, sometime soon after, the news will be out. We don't want our visitors attacked by mobs drunk on superstition, planetary isolation, or any other form of tabloid hysteria. We don't want them carrying stories back to their civilization of being shot at by a suspendered fanatic who screamed, 'Go back where you come from, you furrin seafood!' We want to give them the impression that we are a fairly amiable, fairly intelligent race, that we can be dealt with reasonably well."

I nodded. "Yeah. So they'll set up trading posts on this planet instead of garrisons. But what do I do in all this?"

He punched my chest gently. "You, Dick — you do a job of public relations. You sell these aliens to the American people!"

The official had maneuvered around in front of me. I recognized him. He was the Undersecretary of State.

"Would you step this way, please?" he said. "I'd like to introduce you to our distinguished guests."

So he stepped, and I stepped, and we scrunched across the field and clanked across the steel plate and stood next to our gastropodic guests.

"Ahem," said the Undersecretary politely.

The nearer snail bent an eye toward us. The other eye drew a bead on the companion snail, and then the great slimy head arched and came down to our level. The creature raised, as it were, one cheek of its foot and said, with all the mellowness of air being pumped through a torn inner tube, "Can it be that you wish to communicate with my unworthy self, respected sir?"

I was introduced. The thing brought two eyes to bear on me. The place where its chin should have been dropped to my feet and snaked around there for a second. Then it said, "You, honored sir, are our touchstone, the link with all that is great in your noble race. Your condescension is truly a tribute."

All this tumbled out while I was muttering "How," and extending a diffident hand. The snail put one eyeball in my palm and the other on the back of my wrist. It didn't shake; it just put the things there and took them away again. I had the wit not to wipe my hands on my pants, which was my immediate impulse. The eyeball wasn't exactly dry, either.

I said, "I'll do my best. Tell me, are you — uh — ambassadors, sort of? Or maybe just explorers?"

"Our small worth justifies no titles," said the creature, "yet we are both; for all communication is ambassadorship of a kind, and any seeker after knowledge is an explorer."

I was suddenly reminded of an old story with the punchline, "Ask a foolish question and you get a foolish answer." I also wondered suddenly what snails eat.

The second alien glided over and eyed me. "You may depend upon our utmost obedience," it said humbly. "We understand your awesome function and we wish to be liked to whatever extent it is possible for your admirable race to like such miserable creatures as ourselves."

"Stick to that attitude and we'll get along," I said.

By and large, they were a pleasure to work with. I mean there was no temperament, no up-staging, no insistence on this camera angle or that mention of a previously published book or the other wishful biographical apocrypha about being raised in a convent, like with most of my other clients.

On the other hand, they weren't easy to talk to. They'd take orders, sure. But ask them a question. Any question:

"How long did the trip take you?"

" 'How long' in your eloquent tongue indicates a frame of reference dealing with duration. I hesitate to discuss so complex a problem with one as learned as yourself. The velocities involved make it necessary to answer in relative terms. Our lowly and undesirable planet recedes from this beauteous system during part of its orbital period, advances toward it during part. Also, we must take into consideration the direction and velocity of our star in reference to the cosmic expansion of this portion of the continuum. Had we come from Cygnus, say, or Bootes, the question could be answered somewhat more directly; for those bodies travel in a contiguous arc skewed from the ecliptic plane in such a way that —"

Or a question like, "Is your government a democracy?"

"A democracy is a rule of the people, according to your rich etymology. We could not, in our lowly tongue, have expressed it so succinctly and movingly. One must govern oneself, of course. The degree of governmental control on the individual must vary from individual to individual and in the individual from time to time. This is so evident to as comprehensive a mind as yours that I trust you forgive me my inanities. The same control applies, naturally, to individuals considered in the mass. When faced with a universal necessity, the tendency exists among civilized species to unite to fill the need. Therefore, when no such necessity exists, there is less reason for concerted effort. Since this applies to all species, it applies even to such as us. On the other hand—"

See what I mean? A little of that got old quickly with me. I was happy to keep my nose to my own grindstone.

The Government gave me a month for the preparatory propaganda. Originally, the story was to break in two weeks, but I got down on my hands and knees and bawled that a publicity deadline required at least five times that. So they gave me a month.

Explain that carefully, Alvarez. I want them to understand exactly what a job I faced. All those years of lurid magazine covers showing extremely nubile females being menaced in three distinct colors by assorted monstrosities; those horror movies, those invasion-from-outer-space novels, those Sunday supplement fright splashes — all those sturdy psychological ruts I had to retrack. Not to mention the shudders elicited by mention of "worms," the regulation distrust of even human "furriners," the superstitious dread of creatures who had no visible place to park a soul.

Trowson helped me round up the men to write the scientific articles, and I dug up the boys who could pseudo them satisfactorily. Magazine mats were ripped apart to make way for yarns speculating gently on how far extraterrestrial races might have evolved beyond us, how much more ethical they might have become, how imaginary seven-headed creatures could still apply the Sermon on the Mount. Syndicated features popped up describing "Humble Creatures Who Create Our Gardens," "Snail Racing, the Spectacular New Spectator Sport," and so much stuff on "The Basic Unity of All Living Things" that I began to get uncomfortable at even a vegetarian dinner. I remember hearing there was a perceptible boom in mineral waters and vitamin pills. . . .

And all this, mind you, without a word of the real story breaking. A columnist did run a cute and cryptic item about someone having finally found meat on the flying saucers, but half an hour of earnest discussion in an abandoned finger-print file room prejudiced him against further comment along this line.

The video show was the biggest problem. I don't think I could have done it on time with anything less than the resources and influence of the United States Government behind me. But a week before the official announcement, I had both the video show and the comic strip in production.

I think fourteen — though maybe it was more — of the country's best comedy writers collaborated on the project, not to mention the horde of illustrators and university psychologists who combined to sweat out the delightful little drawings. We used the drawings as the basis for the puppets on the TV show and I don't think anything was ever so gimmicked up with Popular Appeal — and I do mean *Popular* — as "Andy and Dandy."

Those two fictional snails crept into the heart of America like a virus infection: overnight, everybody was talking about their anthropomorphic antics, repeating their quotable running gags and adjuring each other not to miss the next show. ("You *can't* miss it, Steve; it's on every channel anyway. Right after supper.") I had the tie-ins, too: Andy and Dandy dolls for the girls, snail scooters for the boys, everything from pictures on cocktail glasses to kitchen decalcomanias. Of course, a lot of the tie-ins didn't come off the production line till after the Big Announcement.

When we gave the handouts to the newspapers, we "suggested" what headlines to use. They had a choice of ten. Even *The New York Times* was forced to shriek "REAL ANDY AND DANDY BLOW IN FROM BETELGEUSE," and under that a four-column cut of blond Baby Ann Joyce with the snails.

Baby Ann had been flown out from Hollywood for the photograph. The cut showed her standing between the two aliens and clutching an eye stalk of each in her trusting, chubby hands.

The nicknames stuck. Those two slimy intellectuals from another star became even more important than the youthful evangelist who was currently being sued for bigamy.

Andy and Dandy had a ticker-tape reception in New York. They obligingly laid a cornerstone for the University of Chicago's new library. They posed for the newsreels everywhere, surrounded by Florida oranges, Idaho potatoes, Milwaukee beer. They were magnificently cooperative.

From time to time I wondered what they thought of us. They had no facial expressions, which was scarcely odd, since they had no faces. Their long eye stalks swung this way and that as they rode down shrieking Broadway in the back seat of the mayor's car; their gelatinous body-foot would heave periodically and the mouth under it make a smacking noise, but when the photographers suggested that they curl around the barely clad beauties, the time video rigged up a Malibu Beach show, Andy and Dandy wriggled over and complied without a word. Which is more than I can say for the barely clad beauties.

And when the winning pitcher presented them with an autographed baseball at that year's World Series, they bowed gravely, their pink shell tops glistening in the sunlight, and said throatily into the battery of microphones: "We're the happiest fans in the universe!"

The country went wild over them.

"But we can't keep them here," Trowson predicted. "Did you read about the debate in the U.N. General Assembly yesterday? We are accused of making secret alliances with non-human aggressors against the best interests of our own species."

I shrugged. "Well, let them go overseas. I don't think anyone else will be more successful extracting information from them than we were."

Professor Trowson wriggled his short body up on a corner of his desk. He lifted a folderful of typewritten notes and grimaced as if his tongue were wrapped in wool.

"Four months of careful questioning," he grumbled. "Four

months of painstaking interrogation by trained sociologists using every free moment the aliens had, which admittedly wasn't much. Four months of organized investigation, of careful data sifting." He dropped the folder disgustedly to the desk and some of the pages splashed out. "And we know more about the social structure of Atlantis than Betelgeuse IX."

We were in the wing of the Pentagon assigned to what the brass hats, in their own cute way, had christened Project Encyclopedia. I strolled across the large, sunny office and glanced at the very latest organizational wall chart. I pointed to a small rectangle labeled "Power Source Sub-Section" depending via a straight line from a larger rectangle marked "Alien Physical Science Inquiry Section." In the small rectangle, very finely printed, were the names of an army major, a WAC corporal, and Drs. Lopez, Vinthe, and Mainzer.

"How're they doing?" I asked.

"Not much better, I'm afraid." Trowson turned away with a sigh from peering over my shoulder. "At least I deduce that from the unhappy way Mainzer bubbles into his soup spoon at lunch. Conversation between sub-sections originating in different offices on the departmental level is officially discouraged, you know. But I remember Mainzer from the university cafeteria. He bubbled into his soup the very same way when he was stuck on his solar refraction engine."

"Think Andy and Dandy are afraid we're too young to play with matches? Or maybe apelike creatures are too unpleasant-looking to be allowed to circulate in their refined and esthetic civilization?"

"I don't *know*, Dick." The prof ambled back to his desk and leafed irritably through his sociological notes. "If anything like that is true, why would they give us free run of their ship? Why would they reply so gravely and courteously to every question? If only their answers weren't so vague in our terms! But they are such complex and artistically minded creatures, so chockful of poetic sentiment and good manners that it's impossible to make mathematical or even verbal sense out of their vast and circumlocutory explanations. Sometimes, when I think of their highly polished manners and their seeming lack of interest in the structure of their society, when I put that together with their spaceship, which looks like one of those tiny jade carvings that took a lifetime to accomplish —"

He trailed off and began riffling the pages like a Mississippi steamboat gambler going over somebody else's deck of cards.

"Isn't it possible we just don't have enough stuff as yet to understand them?"

"Yes. In fact, that's what we always come back to. Warbury points to the tremendous development in our language since the advent of technical vocabularies. He says that this process, just beginning with us, already affects our conceptual approach as well as our words. And, naturally, in a race so much further along — But if we could only find a science of theirs which bears a faint resemblance to one of ours!"

I felt sorry for him, standing there blinking futilely out of gentle, academic eyes.

"Cheer up, Prof. Maybe by the time old Suckfoot and his pal come back from the Grand Tour, you'll have unsnarled a sophistry and we'll be off this 'Me, friend; you come from across sea in great bird with many wings' basis that we seem to have wandered into."

And there you are, Alvarez: a cheap advertising small-brain like me, and I was that close. I should have said something then. Bet you wouldn't have nodded at me heavily and said, "I hope so, Dick. I desperately hope so." But, come to think of it, not only Trowson was trotting up that path. So was Warbury. So were Lopez, Vinthe, and Mainzer. So was I, among others.

I had a chance to relax when Andy and Dandy went abroad. My job wasn't exactly over, but the public relations end was meshing right along, with me needed only once in a while to give a supervisory spin. Chiefly, I maintained close contact with my opposite number in various other sovereign states, giving out with experienced advice on how to sell the Boys from Betelgeuse. They had to adjust it to their own mass phobias and popular myths; but they were a little happier about it than I had been without any clear idea of what public behavior to expect of our visitors.

Remember, when *I'd* started, I hadn't even been sure those snails were housebroken.

I followed them in the newspapers. I pasted the pictures of the Mikado receiving them next to their nice comments on the Taj Mahal. They weren't nearly so nice to the Akhund of Swat, but then when you think of what the Akhund said about them . . .

They tended to do that everywhere, giving just a little better than they got. For example, when they were presented with those newly created decorations in Red Square (Dandy got the Order of Extraterrestrial Friends of Soviet Labor, while, for some abstruse reason, the Order of Heroic Interstellar Champion of the Soviet People was conferred upon Andy), they came out with a long, ringing speech about the scientific validity of communist government. It made for cheering, flower-tossing crowds in the Ukraine and Poland but a certain amount of restiveness in these United States.

But before I had to run my staff into overtime hours, whipping up press releases which recapitulated the aliens' statement before the joint houses of Congress and their lovely, sentimental comments at Valley Forge, the aliens were in Berne, telling the Swiss that only free enterprise could have produced the yodel, the Incabloc escapement in watches, and such a superb example of liberty; hadn't they had democracy long enough to have had it first, and wasn't it wonderful?

By the time they reached Paris I had the national affection pretty much under control again, although here and there a tabloid still muttered peevishly in its late city final. But, as always, Andy and Dandy put the clincher on. Even then I wondered whether they really liked DeRoges's latest abstraction for itself alone.

But they bought the twisted sculpture, paying for it, since they had no cash of their own, with a thumb-sized gadget which actually melted marble to any degree of pattern delicacy the artist desired, merely by being touched to the appropriate surface. DeRoges threw away his chisels blissfully, but six of the finest minds in France retired to intensive nervous breakdowns after a week of trying to solve the tool's working principles.

It went over big here:

ANDY AND DANDY
PASS AS THEY GO

Betelgeuse Businessmen
Show Appreciation
for Value Received.

This newspaper notes with pleasure the sound shopper's ethics behind the latest transaction of our distinguished guests from the elemental void. Understanding the inexorable law of supply and demand, these representatives of an advanced economic system refuse to succumb to the "gimmies." If certain other members of the human race were to examine carefully the true implications of . . .

So when they returned to the United States after being presented at the British court, they got juicy spreads in all the newspapers, a tug-whistle reception in New York harbor and the mayor's very chiefest deputy there on City Hall steps to receive them.

And even though people were more or less accustomed to

them now, they were somehow never shoved off page one. There was the time a certain furniture polish got a testimonial out of them in which the aliens announced that they'd had particularly happy and glossy results on their tiny shell toppers with the goo; and they used the large financial rewards of the testimonial to buy ten extremely rare orchids and have them sunk in plastic. And there was the time . . .

I missed the television show on which it broke. I had gone to a side-street movie theater that night to see a revival of one of my favorite Chaplin pictures; and I'd never enjoyed the ostentatious greet-the-great hysterics of *Celebrity Salon* anyway. I hadn't any idea of how long the M.C., Bill Bancroft, had waited to get Andy and Dandy on his program, and how much he was determined to make it count when the big night arrived.

Reconstructed and stripped of meaningless effusion, it went something like this:

Bancroft asked them if they weren't anxious to get home to the wife and kiddies. Andy explained patiently, for perhaps the thirty-fourth time, that, since they were hermaphrodites, they had no family in any humanly acceptable sense. Bancroft cut into the explanation to ask them what ties they *did* have. Chiefly the revitalizer, says Andy politely.

Revitalizer? What's a revitalizer? Oh, a machine they have to expose themselves to every decade or so, says Dandy. There's at least one revitalizer in every large city on their home planet.

Bancroft makes a bad pun, waits for the uproarious audience to regain control, then asks: And this revitalizer — just what does it do? Andy goes into a long-winded explanation, the gist of which is that the revitalizers stir up cytoplasm in animal cells and refresh them.

I see, cracks Bancroft; the pause every decade that refreshes. And then, after being refreshed, you have what as a result? "Oh," muses Dandy, "you might say we have no fear of cancer or any degenerative disease. Besides that, by exposing ourselves to revitalizers at regular intervals throughout our lifetime and refreshing our body cells, we quintuple our life expectancy. We live five times longer than we should. That's about what the revitalizer does, you might say," says Dandy. Andy, after thinking a bit, agrees. "That's about it."

Pandemonium, and not mild. Newspaper extras in all languages, including the Scandinavian. Lights burning late at night in the U.N. Headquarters with guards twenty deep around the site.

When President of the Assembly Sadhu asked them why they'd never mentioned revitalizers before, they did the snail equivalent of shrugging and said the Betelgeuse IX equivalent of nobody ever asked them.

President Sadhu cleared his throat, waved all complications aside with his long brown fingers and announced, "That is not important. Not now. We must have revitalizers."

It seemed to take the aliens awhile to understand that. When they finally became convinced that we, as a species, were utterly entranced with the prospect of two to four centuries of life instead of fifty or sixty years, they went into a huddle.

But their race didn't make these machines for export, they explained regretfully. Just enough to service their population. And while they *could* see as how we might like and must obviously deserve to have these gadgets, there was none to ferry back from Betelgeuse.

Sadhu didn't even look around for advice. "What would your people want?" he asked. "What would they like in exchange for manufacturing these machines for us? We will pay almost any price within the power of this entire planet." A rumbling, eager "yes" in several languages rolled across the floor of the Assembly.

Andy and Dandy couldn't think of a thing. Sadhu begged

them to try. He personally escorted them to their spaceship, which was now parked in a restricted area in Central Park. "Good night, gentlemen," said President of the Assembly Sadhu. "Try — please try hard to think of an exchange."

They stayed inside their ship for almost six days while the world almost went insane with impatience. When I think of all the fingernails bitten that week by two billion people . . .

"Imagine!" Trowson whispered to me. He was pacing the floor as if he fully intended to walk all the way to Betelgeuse. "We'd just be children on a quintupled life scale, Dick. All my achievement and education, all yours, would be just the beginning! A man could learn five professions in such a life — and think what he could accomplish in one!"

I nodded, a little numb. I was thinking of the books I could read, the books I might write, if the bulk of my life stretched ahead of me and the advertising profession was just a passing phase at the beginning of it. Then again, somehow I'd never married, never had had a family. Not enough free time, I had felt. And now, at forty, I was too set in my ways. But a man can unset a lot in a century . . .

In six days the aliens came out. With a statement of price.

They believed they could persuade their people to manufacture a supply of revitalizers for us if — An IF writ very large indeed.

Their planet was woefully short of radioactive minerals, they explained apologetically. Barren worlds containing radium, uranium, and thorium had been discovered and claimed by other races, but the folk of Betelgeuse IX were forbidden by their ethics to wage aggressive war for territorial purposes. We had plenty of radioactive ore, which we used chiefly for war and biological research. The former was patently undesirable and the latter would be rendered largely unnecessary by the revitalizers.

So, in exchange, they wanted our radioactive elements. All of them, they stated humbly.

All right, we were a little surprised, even stunned. But the protests never *started* to materialize. There was an overwhelming chorus of "sold!" from every quadrant of the globe. A couple of generals here, a few militaristic statesmen there managed to raise direly pointing forefingers before they were whisked out of position. A nuclear physicist or two howled about the future of subatomic research, but the peoples of the earth howled louder.

"Research? How much research can you do in a lifetime of three hundred years?"

Overnight, the United Nations became the central office of a planet-wide mining concession. National boundaries were superseded by pitchblende deposits and swords were beaten into pickaxes. Practically anyone with a good, usable arm enlisted in the shovel brigades for two or more months out of the year. Camaraderie flew on the winds of the world.

Andy and Dandy politely offered to help. They marked out on detail contour maps the spots to be mined, and that included areas never suspected of radioactivity. They supplied us with fantastic but clear line drawings of devices for extracting the stuff from the ores in which it assayed poorly, and taught us the exact use of these devices, if not their basic principle.

They hadn't been joking. They wanted it all.

Then, when everything was running smoothly, they buzzed off for Betelgeuse to handle their part of the bargain.

Those two years were the most exhilarating of my life. And I'd say everyone feels the same, don't they, Alvarez? The knowledge that the world was working together, cheerfully, happily, for life itself. I put *my* year in at the Great Slave Lake, and I don't think anyone of my age and weight lifted more pitchblende.

Andy and Dandy came back in two huge ships, manned by weird snail-like robots. The robots did everything, while

Andy and Dandy went on being lionized. From the two ships, almost covering the sky, the robots ferried back and forth in strange, spiral aircraft, bringing revitalizers down, carrying refined radioactive elements aloft. No one paid the slightest attention to their methods of instantaneous extraction from large quantities of ore: we were interested in just one throbbing thought — the revitalizers.

They worked. And that, so far as most of us were concerned, was that.

The revitalizers *worked*. Cancer disappeared; heart disease and kidney disease became immediately arrested. Insects which were introduced into the square one-story lab structures lived for a year instead of a few months. And humans — doctors shook their heads in wonder over people who had gone through.

All over the planet, near every major city, the long, patient, slowly moving lines stood outside the revitalizers, which were rapidly becoming something else.

"Temples!" shouted Mainzer. "They look on them as temples. A scientist investigating their operation is treated by the attendants like a dangerous lunatic in a nursery. Not that a man can find a clue in those ridiculously small motors. I no longer ask what their power source can be. Instead, I ask if they have a power source at *all*!"

"The revitalizers are very precious now, in the beginning," Trowson soothed him. "After a while the novelty will wear off and you'll be able to investigate at your leisure. Could it be solar power?"

"No!" Mainzer shook his huge head positively. "Not solar power. Solar power I am sure I could recognize. As I am sure that the power supply of their ships and whatever runs these — these revitalizers are two entirely separate things. On the ships I have given up. But the revitalizers I believe I could solve. If only they would let me examine them. Fools! So terribly afraid I might damage one, and they would have to travel to another city for their elixir!"

We patted his shoulder, but we weren't really interested. Andy and Dandy left that week, after wishing us well in their own courteous and complex fashion. Whole population groups blew kisses at their mineral-laden ships.

Six months after they left, the revitalizers stopped.

"Am I certain?" Trowson snorted at my dismayed face. "One set of statistics proves it: look at your death rate. It's back to pre-Betelgeuse normal. Or ask any doctor. Any doctor who can forget his U.N. security oath, that is. There'll be really wild riots when the news breaks, Dick."

"But *why*?" I asked him. "Did we do something wrong?"

He started a laugh that ended with his teeth clicking frightenedly together. He rose and walked to the window, staring out into the star-diseased sky. "We did something wrong, all right. We trusted. We made the same mistake all natives have made when they met a superior civilization. Mainzer and Lopez have taken one of the revitalizer engine units apart. There was just a trace of it left, but this time they found the power source. Dick, my boy, the revitalizers were run on the fuel of completely pure radioactive elements!"

I needed a few moments to file that properly. Then I sat down in the easy chair very, very carefully. I made some hoarse, improbable sounds before croaking: "Prof, do you mean they wanted that stuff for themselves, for their own revitalizers? That everything they did on this planet was carefully planned so that they could con us with a maximum of friendliness all around? It doesn't seem — it just can't — Why, with their superior science, they could have conquered us if they'd cared to. They could have —"

"No, they couldn't have," Trowson whipped out. He turned to face me and flung his arms across each other. "They're a decadent, dying race; they wouldn't have attempted to conquer us. Not because of their ethics — this huge, horrible swindle serves to illustrate *that* aspect of them — but because they haven't the energy, the concentration, the interest. Andy and Dandy are probably representative of the few remaining who have barely enough git-up-and-go to *trick* backward peoples out of the all-important, life-sustaining revitalizer fuel."

The implications were just beginning to soak into my cortex. Me, the guy who did the most complete and colossal public-relations job of all time — I could just see what my relations with the public would be like if I was ever connected with this shambles.

"And without atomic power, Prof, we won't have space travel!"

He gestured bitterly. "Oh, we've been taken, Dick; the whole human race has been had. I know what you're going through, but think of me! I'm the failure, the man responsible. I'm supposed to be a sociologist! How could I have missed? *How?* It was all there: the lack of interest in their own culture, the overintellectualization of esthetics, the involved methods of thought and expression, the exaggerated etiquette, even the very first thing of theirs we saw — their ship — was too heavily stylized and intricately designed for a young, trusting civilization.

"They *had* to be decadent; every sign pointed to that conclusion. And of course the fact that they resort to the methods of fueling their revitalizers that we've experienced — when if we had their science, what might we not do, what substitutes might we not develop! No wonder they couldn't explain their science to us; I doubt if they understand it fully themselves. They are the profligate, inadequate and sneak-thief heirs of what was once a soaring race!"

I was following my own unhappy images. "And we're still hicks. Hicks who've been sold the equivalent of the Brooklyn Bridge by some dressed-up sharpies from Betelgeuse."

Trowson nodded. "Or a bunch of poor natives who have

sold their island home to a group of European explorers for a handful of brightly colored glass beads."

But of course we were both wrong, Alvarez. Neither Trowson nor I had figured on Mainzer or Lopez or the others. Like Mainzer said, a few years earlier and we would have been licked. But man had entered the atomic age some time before 1945 and people like Mainzer and Vinthe had done nuclear research back in the days when radioactive elements abounded on Earth. We had that and we had such tools as the cyclotron, the betatron. And, if our present company will pardon the expression, Alvarez, we are a young and vigorous race.

All we had to do was the necessary research.

The research was done. With a truly effective world government, with a population not only interested in the problem but recently experienced in working together — and with the grim incentive we had, Alvarez, the problem, as you know, was solved.

We developed artificial radioactives and refueled the revitalizers. We developed atomic fuels out of the artificial radioactives and we got space travel. We did it comparatively fast, and we weren't interested in a ship that just went to the Moon or Mars. We wanted a star ship. And we wanted it so bad, so fast, that we have it now too.

Here we are. Explain the situation to them, Alvarez, just the way I told it to you, but with all the knee-bending and gobbledegook that a transplanted Brazilian with twelve years Oriental trading experience can put into it. You're the man to do it — I can't talk like that. It's the only language those decadent slugs understand, so it's the only way we can talk to them. So talk to them, these slimy snails, these oysters on the quarter shell, those smart-alecky slugs. Don't forget to mention to them that the supply of radioactives they got from us won't last forever. Get that down in fine detail.

Then stress the fact that we've got artificial radioactives, and that they've got some things we know we want and lots of other things we mean to find out about.

Tell them, Alvarez, that we've come to collect tolls on that Brooklyn Bridge they sold us.

Ellis Konigswasser thought human bodies were a lot more trouble than they were worth. He wished people could live outside their bodies. In this story, master satirist Kurt Vonnegut explores what happens when Konigswasser's wish comes true.

UNREADY TO WEAR

KURT VONNEGUT, JR.

I don't suppose the oldsters, those of us who weren't born into it, will ever feel quite at home being amphibious — amphibious in the new sense of the word. I still catch myself feeling blue about things that don't matter anymore.

I can't help worrying about my business, for instance — or what used to be my business. After all, I spent thirty years building the thing up from scratch, and now the equipment is rusting and getting clogged with dirt. But even though I know it's silly of me to care what happens to the business, I borrow a body from a storage center every so often, and go around the old hometown, and clean and oil as much of the equipment as I can.

Of course, all in the world the equipment was good for was making money, and Lord knows there's plenty of that lying around. Not as much as there used to be, because there at first some people got frisky and threw it all around, and the wind blew it every which way. And a lot of go-getters gathered up piles of the stuff and hid it somewhere. I hate to admit it, but I gathered up close to a half million myself and stuck it away. I used to get it out and count it sometimes, but that was years ago. Right now I'd be hard put to say where it is.

But the worrying I do about my old business is bush-league stuff compared to the worrying my wife, Madge, does about our old house. That thing is what she herself put in thirty years on while I was building the business. Then no sooner had we gotten nerve enough to build and decorate the place than everybody we cared anything about got amphibious. Madge borrows a body once a month and dusts the place, though the only thing a house is good for now is keeping termites and mice from getting pneumonia.

Whenever it's my turn to get into a body and work as an attendant at the local storage center, I realize all over again how much tougher it is for women to get used to being amphibious.

Madge borrows bodies a lot oftener than I do, and that's true of women in general. We have to keep three times as many women's bodies in stock as men's bodies, in order to meet the demand. Every so often, it seems as though a woman just *has* to have a body, and doll it up in clothes, and look at herself in a mirror. And Madge, God bless her, I don't think she'll be satisfied until she's tried on every body in every storage center on Earth.

It's been a fine thing for Madge, though. I never kid her about it, because it's done so much for her personality. Her old body, to tell you the plain blunt truth, wasn't anything to get excited about, and having to haul the thing around made her gloomy a lot of the times in the old days. She couldn't help it, poor soul, any more than anybody else could help what sort of body they'd been born with, and I loved her in spite of it.

Well, after we'd learned to be amphibious, and after we'd built the storage centers and laid in body supplies and opened them to the public, Madge went hog wild. She borrowed a platinum blonde body that had been donated by a burlesque queen, and I didn't think we'd ever get her out of it. As I say, it did wonders for her self-confidence.

I'm like most men and don't care particularly what body

I get. Just the strong, good-looking, healthy bodies were put in storage, so one is as good as the next one. Sometimes, when Madge and I take bodies out together for old times' sake, I let her pick out one for me to match whatever she's got on. It's a funny thing how she always picks a blond, tall one for me.

My old body, which she claims she loved for a third of a century, had black hair, and was short and paunchy, too, there toward the last. I'm human and I couldn't help being hurt when they scrapped it after I'd left it, instead of putting it in storage. It was a good, homey, comfortable body; nothing fast and flashy, but reliable. But there isn't much call for that kind of body at the centers, I guess. I never ask for one, at any rate.

The worst experience I ever had with a body was when I was flimflammed into taking out the one that had belonged to Dr. Ellis Konigswasser. It belongs to the Amphibious Pioneers' Society and only gets taken out once a year for the big Pioneers' Day Parade, on the anniversary of Konigswasser's discovery. Everybody said it was a great honor for me to be picked to get into Konigswasser's body and lead the parade.

Like a plain damn fool, I believed them.

They'll have a tough time getting me into that thing again — ever. Taking that wreck out certainly made it plain why Konigswasser discovered how people could do without their bodies. That old one of his practically *drives* you out. Ulcers, headaches, arthritis, fallen arches — a nose like a pruning hook, piggy little eyes, and a complexion like a used steamer trunk. He was and still is the sweetest person you'd ever want to know, but, back when he was stuck with that body, nobody got close enough to find out.

We tried to get Konigswasser back into his old body to lead us when we first started having the Pioneers' Day Parades, but he wouldn't have anything to do with it, so we always have to flatter some poor boob into taking on the job. Konigswasser marches, all right, but as a six-foot cowboy who can bend beer cans double between his thumb and middle finger.

Konigswasser is just like a kid with that body. He never gets tired of bending beer cans with it, and we all have to stand around in our bodies after the parade, and watch as though we were very impressed.

I don't suppose he could bend very much of anything back in the old days.

Nobody mentions it to him, since he's the grand old man of the Amphibious Age, but he plays hell with the bodies. Almost every time he takes one out, he busts it, showing off. Then somebody has to get into a surgeon's body and sew it up again.

I don't mean to be disrespectful of Konigswasser. As a matter of fact, it's a respectful thing to say that somebody is childish in certain ways, because it's people like that who seem to get all the big ideas.

There is a picture of him in the old days down at the Historical Society, and you can see from that that he never did grow up as far as keeping up his appearance went — doing what little he could with the rattle-trap body Nature had issued him.

His hair was down below his collar, he wore his pants so low that his heels wore through the legs above the cuffs, and the lining of his coat hung down in festoons all around the bottom. And he'd forget meals, and go out into the cold or wet without enough clothes on, and he would never notice sickness until it almost killed him. He was what we used to call absentminded. Looking back now, of course, we say he was starting to be amphibious.

Konigswasser was a mathematician, and he did all his living with his mind. The body he had to haul around with that wonderful mind was about as much use to him as a flatcar of scrap iron. Whenever he got sick and *had* to pay some attention to his body, he'd rant somewhat like this:

"The mind is the only thing about human beings that's worth anything. Why does it have to be tied to a bag of skin, blood, hair, meat, bones, and tubes? No wonder people can't get anything done, stuck for life with a parasite that has to be stuffed with food and protected from weather and germs all the time. And the fool thing wears out anyway — no matter how much you stuff and protect it!

"Who," he wanted to know, "really wants one of the things? What's so wonderful about protoplasm that we've got to carry so damned many pounds of it with us wherever we go?

"Trouble with the world," said Konigswasser, "isn't too many people — it's too many bodies."

When his teeth went bad on him, and he had to have them all out, and he couldn't get a set of dentures that were at all comfortable, he wrote in his diary, "If living matter was able to evolve enough to get out of the ocean, which was really quite a pleasant place to live, it certainly ought to be able to take another step and get out of bodies, which are pure nuisances when you stop to think about them."

He wasn't a prude about bodies, understand, and he wasn't jealous of people who had better ones than he did. He just thought bodies were a lot more trouble than they were worth.

He didn't have great hopes that people would really evolve out of their bodies in his time. He just wished they would. Thinking hard about it, he walked through a park in his shirtsleeves and stopped off at the zoo to watch the lions being fed. Then, when the rainstorm turned to sleet, he headed back home and was interested to see firemen on the edge of a lagoon, where they were using a Pulmotor on a drowned man.

Witnesses said the old man had walked right into the water and had kept going without changing his expression until he'd disappeared. Konigswasser got a look at the victim's face and said he'd never seen a better reason for suicide. He started for home again and was almost there before he realized that that was his own body lying back there.

He went back to reoccupy the body just as the firemen got it breathing again, and he walked it home, more as a favor to the city than anything else. He walked it into his front closet, got out of it again, and left it there.

He took it out only when he wanted to do some writing or turn the pages of a book, or when he had to feed it so it would have enough energy to do the few odd jobs he gave it. The rest of the time, it sat motionless in the closet, looking dazed and using almost no energy. Konigswasser told me the other day that he used to run the thing for about a dollar a week, just taking it out when he really needed it.

But the best part was that Konigswasser didn't have to sleep anymore, just because *it* had to sleep; or be afraid anymore, just because *it* thought it might get hurt; or go looking for things *it* seemed to think it had to have. And, when *it* didn't feel well, Konigswasser kept out of it until it felt better, and he didn't have to spend a fortune keeping the thing comfortable.

When he got his body out of the closet to write, he did a book on how to get out of one's own body, which was rejected without comment by twenty-three publishers. The twenty-fourth sold two million copies, and the book changed human life more than the invention of fire, numbers, the alphabet, agriculture, or the wheel. When somebody told Konigswasser that, he snorted that they were damning his book with faint praise. I'd say he had a point there.

By following the instructions in Konigswasser's book for about two years, almost anybody could get out of his body whenever he wanted to. The first step was to understand what a parasite and dictator the body was most of the time, then to separate what the body wanted or didn't want from what you yourself — your psyche — wanted or didn't want. Then, by concentrating on what you wanted, and ignoring as much as possible what the body wanted beyond plain maintenance, you made your psyche demand its right and become self-sufficient.

That's what Konigswasser had done without realizing it, until he and his body had parted company in the park, with his psyche going to watch the lions eat, and with his body wandering out of control into the lagoon.

The final trick of separation, once your psyche grew independent enough, was to start your body walking in some direction and suddenly take your psyche off in another direction. You couldn't do it standing still, for some reason — you had to walk.

At first, Madge's and my psyches were clumsy at getting along outside our bodies, like the first sea animals that got stranded on land millions of years ago, and who could just waddle and squirm and gasp in the mud. But we became better at it with time, because the psyche can naturally adapt so much faster than the body.

Madge and I had good reasons for wanting to get out. Everybody who was crazy enough to try to get out at the first had good reasons. Madge's body was sick and wasn't going to last a lot longer. With her going in a little while, I couldn't work up enthusiasm for sticking around much longer myself. So we studied Konigswasser's book and tried to get Madge out of her body before it died. I went along with her, to keep either one of us from getting lonely. And we just barely made it — six weeks before her body went all to pieces.

That's why we get to march every year in the Pioneer's Day Parade. Not everybody does — only the first five thousand of us who turned amphibious. We were guinea pigs, without much to lose one way or another, and we were the ones who proved to the rest how pleasant and safe it was — a heck of a lot safer than taking chances in a body year in and year out.

Sooner or later, almost everybody had a good reason for giving it a try. There got to be millions and finally more than a billion of us — invisible, insubstantial, indestructible, and, by golly, true to ourselves, no trouble to anybody, and not afraid of anything.

When we're not in bodies, the Amphibious Pioneers can meet on the head of a pin. When we get into bodies for the Pioneers' Day Parade, we take up over fifty thousand square feet, have to gobble more than three tons of food to get enough energy to march; and lots of us catch colds or worse, and get sore because somebody's body accidentally steps on the heel of somebody else's body, and get jealous because some bodies get to lead and others have to stay in ranks, and — oh, hell, I don't know what all.

I'm not crazy about the parade. With all of us there, close together in bodies — well, it brings out the worst in us, no matter how good our psyches are. Last year, for instance, Pioneers' Day was a scorcher. People couldn't help being out of sorts, stuck in sweltering, thirsty bodies for hours.

Well, one thing led to another, and the Parade Marshal offered to beat the daylights out of my body with his body, if my body got out of step again. Naturally, being Parade Marshal, he had the best body that year, except for Konigswasser's cowboy, but I told him to soak his fat head, anyway. He swung, and I ditched my body right there, and didn't even stick around long enough to find out if he connected. He had to haul my body back to the storage center himself.

I stopped being mad at him the minute I got out of the

body. I understood, you see. Nobody but a saint could be really sympathetic or intelligent for more than a few minutes at a time in a body — or happy, either, except in short spurts. I haven't met an amphibian yet who wasn't easy to get along with, and cheerful and interesting — as long as he was outside a body. And I haven't met one yet who didn't turn a little sour when he got into one.

The minute you get in, chemistry takes over — glands making you excitable or ready to fight or hungry or mad or affectionate, or — well, you never know *what's* going to happen next.

That's why I can't get sore at the enemy, the people who are against the amphibians. They never get out of their bodies and won't try to learn. They don't want anybody else to do it, either, and they'd like to make the amphibians get back into bodies and stay in them.

After the tussle I had with the Parade Marshal, Madge got wind of it and left *her* body right in the middle of the Ladies' Auxiliary. And the two of us, feeling full of devilment after getting shed of the bodies and the parade, went over to have a look at the enemy.

I'm never keen on going over to look at them. Madge likes to see what the women are wearing. Stuck with their bodies all the time, the enemy women change their clothes and hair and cosmetic styles a lot oftener than we do on the women's bodies in the storage centers.

I don't get much of a kick out of the fashions, and almost everything else you see and hear in enemy territory would bore a plaster statue into moving away.

Usually, the enemy is talking about old-style reproduction, which is the clumsiest, most comical, most inconvenient thing anyone could imagine, compared with what the amphibians have in that line. If they aren't talking about that, then they're talking about food, the gobs of chemicals they have to stuff into their bodies. Or they'll talk about fear, which we used to call politics — job politics, social politics, government politics.

The enemy hates that, having us able to peek in on them any time we want to, while they can't even see us unless we get into bodies. They seem to be scared to death of us, though being scared of amphibians makes as much sense as being scared of the sunrise. They could have the whole world, except the storage centers, for all the amphibians care. But they bunch together as though we were going to come whooping out of the sky and do something terrible to them at any moment.

They've got contraptions all over the place that are supposed to detect amphibians. The gadgets aren't worth a nickel, but they seem to make the enemy feel good — like they were lined up against great forces, but keeping their nerve and doing important, clever things about it. Know-how — all the time they're patting each other about how much know-how they've got, and about how we haven't got anything by comparison. If know-how means weapons, they're dead right.

I guess there is a war on between them and us. But we never do anything about holding up our side of the war, except to keep our parade sites and our storage centers secret, and to get out of bodies every time there's an air raid, or the enemy fires a rocket, or something.

That just makes the enemy madder, because the raids and rockets and all cost plenty, and blowing up things nobody needs anyway is a poor return on the taxpayers' money. We always know what they're going to do next, and when and where, so there isn't any trick to keeping out of their way.

But they are pretty smart, considering they've got bodies to look after besides doing their thinking, so I always try to be cautious when I go over to watch them. That's why I wanted to clear out when Madge and I saw a storage center in the middle of one of their fields. We hadn't talked to anybody lately about what the enemy was up to, and the center looked awfully suspicious.

Madge was optimistic, the way she's been ever since she borrowed that burlesque queen's body, and she said the storage center was a sure sign that the enemy had seen the light, that they were getting ready to become amphibious themselves.

Well, it looked like it. There was a brand-new center, stocked with bodies and open for business, as innocent as you please. We circled it several times, and Madge's circles got smaller and smaller, as she tried to get a close look at what they had in the way of ladies' ready-to-wear.

"Let's beat it," I said.

"I'm just looking," said Madge. "No harm in looking."

Then she saw what was in the main display case, and she forgot where she was or where she'd come from.

The most striking woman's body I'd ever seen was in the case — six feet tall and built like a goddess. But that wasn't the payoff. The body had copper-colored skin, chartreuse hair and fingernails, and a gold lamé evening gown. Beside that body was the body of a blond, male giant in a pale blue field marshal's uniform, piped in scarlet and spangled with medals.

I think the enemy must have swiped the bodies in a raid on one of our outlying storage centers, and padded and dyed them, and dressed them up.

"Madge, come back!" I said.

The copper-colored woman with the chartreuse hair moved. A siren screamed and soldiers rushed from hiding places to grab the body Madge was in.

The center was a trap for amphibians!

The body Madge hadn't been able to resist had its ankles tied together, so Madge couldn't take the few steps she had to take if she was going to get out of it again.

The soldiers carted her off triumphantly as a prisoner of war. I got into the only body available, the fancy field marshal, to try to help her. It was a hopeless situation, because the field marshal was bait, too, with its ankles tied. The soldiers dragged me after Madge.

The cocky young major in charge of the soldiers did a jig along the shoulder of the road, he was so proud. He was the first man ever to capture an amphibian, which was really something from the enemy's point of view. They'd been at war with us for years, and spent God knows how many billions of dollars, but catching us was the first thing that made any amphibians pay much attention to them.

When we got to the town, people were leaning out of windows and waving their flags, and cheering the soldiers, and hissing Madge and me. Here were all the people who didn't want to be amphibious, who thought it was terrible for anybody to be amphibious — people of all colors, shapes, sizes, and nationalities, joined together to fight the amphibians.

It turned out that Madge and I were going to have a big trial. After being tied up every which way in jail all night, we were taken to a courtroom, where television cameras stared at us.

Madge and I were worn to frazzles, because neither one of us had been cooped up in a body that long since I don't know when. Just when we needed to think more than we ever had, in jail before the trial, the bodies developed hunger pains and we couldn't get them comfortable on the cots, no matter how we tried; and, of course, the bodies just had to have their eight hours sleep.

The charge against us was a capital offense on the books of the enemy — *desertion*. As far as the enemy was concerned, the amphibians had all turned yellow and run out of their bodies, just when their bodies were needed to do brave and important things for humanity.

We didn't have a hope of being acquitted. The only reason there was a trial at all was that it gave them an opportunity to sound off about why they were so right and we were so wrong. The courtroom was jammed with their big brass, all looking angry and brave and noble.

"Mr. Amphibian," said the prosecutor, "you are old enough, aren't you, to remember when all men had to face up to life in their bodies, and work and fight for what they believed in?"

"I remember when the bodies were always getting into fights, and nobody seemed to know why, or how to stop it," I said politely. "The only thing everybody seemed to believe in was that they didn't like to fight."

"What would you say of a soldier who ran away in the face of fire?" he wanted to know.

"I'd say he was scared silly."

"He was helping to lose the battle, wasn't he?"

"Oh, sure." There wasn't any argument on that one.

"Isn't that what the amphibians have done — run out on the human race in the face of the battle of life?"

"Most of us are still alive, if that's what you mean," I said.

It was true. We hadn't licked death, and weren't sure we wanted to, but we'd certainly lengthened life something amazing, compared to the span you could expect in a body.

"You ran out on your responsibilities!" he said.

"Like you'd run out of a burning building, sir," I said.

"Leaving everyone else to struggle on alone!"

"They can all get out the same door that we got out of. You can all get out any time you want to. All you do is figure out what you want and what your body wants, and concentrate on —"

The judge banged his gavel until I thought he'd split it. Here they'd burned every copy of Konigswasser's book they could find, and there I was giving a course in how to get out of a body over a whole television network.

"If you amphibians had your way," said the prosecutor, "everybody would run out on his responsibilities, and let life and progress, as we know them, disappear completely."

"Why, sure," I agreed. "That's the point."

"Men would no longer work for what they believe in?" he challenged.

"I had a friend back in the old days who drilled holes in little square thingamajigs for seventeen years in a factory, and he never did get a very clear idea of what they were for. Another one I knew grew raisins for a glass-blowing company, and the raisins weren't for anybody to eat, and he never did find out why the company bought them. Things like that make me sick — now that I'm in a body, of course — and what I used to do for a living makes me even sicker."

"Then you despise human beings and everything they do," he said.

"I like them fine — better than I ever did before. I just think it's a dirty shame what they have to do to take care of their bodies. You ought to get amphibious and see how happy people can be when they don't have to worry about where their body's next meal is coming from, or how to keep it from freezing in the wintertime, or what's going to happen to them when their body wears out."

"And that, sir, means the end of ambition, the end of greatness!"

"Oh, I don't know what about that," I said. "We've got some pretty great people on our side. They'd be great in *or* out of bodies. It's the end of fear is what it is." I looked right into the lens of the nearest television camera. "And *that's* the most wonderful thing that ever happened to people."

Down came the judge's gavel again, and the brass started to shout me down. The television men turned off their cameras, and all the spectators, except for the biggest brass, were cleared out. I knew I'd really said something. All anybody would be getting on his television set now was organ music.

When the confusion died down, the judge said the trial was over, and that Madge and I were guilty of desertion.

Nothing I could do could get us in any worse, so I talked back.

"Now I understand you poor fish," I said. "You couldn't get along without fear. That's the only skill you've got — how to scare yourselves and other people into doing things. That's the only fun you've got, watching people jump for fear of what you'll do to their bodies or take away from their bodies."

Madge got in her two cents' worth. "The only way you can get any response from anybody is to scare them."

"Contempt of court!" said the judge.

"The only way you can scare people is if you can keep them in their bodies," I told him.

The soldiers grabbed Madge and me and started to drag us out of the courtroom.

"This means war!" I yelled.

Everything stopped right there and the place got very quiet.

"We're already at war," said a general uneasily.

"Well, *we're* not," I answered, "but we will be, if you don't untie Madge and me this instant." I was fierce and impressive in that field marshal's body.

"You haven't any weapons," said the judge, "no know-how. Outside of bodies, amphibians are nothing."

"If you don't cut us loose by the time I count ten," I told him, "the amphibians will occupy the bodies of the whole kit and caboodle of you and march you right off the nearest cliff. The place is surrounded." That was hogwash, of course. Only one person can occupy a body at a time, but the enemy couldn't be sure of that. "One! Two! Three!"

The general swallowed, turned white, and waved his hand vaguely.

"Cut them loose," he said weakly.

The soldiers, terrified, too, were glad to do it. Madge and I were freed.

I took a couple of steps, headed my spirit in another direction, and that beautiful marshal, medals and all, went crashing down the staircase like a grandfather clock.

I realized that Madge wasn't with me. She was still in that copper-colored body with the chartreuse hair and fingernails.

"What's more," I heard her saying, "in payment for all the trouble you've caused us, this body is to be addressed to me at New York, delivered in good condition no later than next Monday."

"Yes, ma'am," said the judge.

When we got home, the Pioneers' Day Parade was just breaking up at the local storage center, and the Parade Marshal got out of his body and apologized to me for acting the way he had.

"Heck, Herb," I said, "you don't need to apologize. You weren't yourself. You were parading around in a body."

That's the best part of being amphibious, next to not being afraid — people forgive you for whatever fool thing you might have done in a body.

Oh, there are drawbacks, I guess, the way there are drawbacks to everything. We still have to work off and on, maintaining the storage centers and getting food to keep the community bodies going. But that's a small drawback, and all the big drawbacks I ever heard of aren't real ones, just old-fashioned thinking by people who can't stop worrying about things they used to worry about before they turned amphibious.

As I say, the oldsters will probably never get really used to it. Every so often, I catch myself getting gloomy over what happened to the pay-toilet business it took me thirty years to build.

But the youngsters don't have any hangovers like that from the past. They don't even worry much about something happening to the storage centers, the way us oldsters do.

So I guess maybe that'll be the next step in evolution — to break clean like those first amphibians who crawled out of the mud into the sunshine, and who never did go back to the sea.

ACKNOWLEDGMENTS *(continued from page 3)*

Clifford D. Simak for "Desertion" by Clifford D. Simak. Copyright ©
1944 by Street & Smith Publications, Inc. Copyright renewed. From THE
ARBOR HOUSE TREASURY OF SCIENCE FICTION MASTERPIECES,
compiled by Robert Silverberg and Martin H. Greenberg.

William Tenn for "Betelgeuse Bridge" by William Tenn. Copyright 1950
by Philip Klass.